Micah's touch scrambled her thoughts.

Her hopes that he hadn't noticed the tremor in her voice faded when he said, "It's going to be okay." He flashed her a smile.

Lost in her despair, she'd failed to see how much power his grins still had to move her, reminding her how they'd laughed together after singings. She realized how much she missed that.

Something else she'd thrown away when she'd tossed him out of her life.

"Tell me the truth, Micah," she blurted. "Why are you helping me?"

"Why wouldn't I? You're pregnant and—"

"You don't have to feel obligated because you're the one who found me."

He shook his head, sadness dimming his eyes. "After all this time, Katie Kay, I thought you knew me better than that."

She winced, realizing how she had wounded him. It hadn't been intentional. She wanted to know the truth about why a man whom she'd treated poorly would help her.

No, it was more than helping. He wanted to be certain she and the *boppli* were taken care of. He was a *gut* man. Better than she deserved.

Jo Ann Brown has always loved stories with happily-ever-after endings. A former military officer, she is thrilled to have the chance to write stories about people falling in love. She is also a photographer and travels with her husband of more than thirty years to places where she can snap pictures. They have three children and live in Florida. Drop her a note at joannbrownbooks.com.

An Amish Proposal

Jo Ann Brown

HARLEQUIN® LOVE INSPIRED®

Recycling programs
for this product may
not exist in your area.

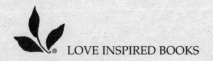

LOVE INSPIRED BOOKS

ISBN-13: 978-0-373-62309-9

An Amish Proposal

Copyright © 2017 by Jo Ann Ferguson

All rights reserved. Except for use in any review, the reproduction or utilization of this work in whole or in part in any form by any electronic, mechanical or other means, now known or hereinafter invented, including xerography, photocopying and recording, or in any information storage or retrieval system, is forbidden without the written permission of the editorial office, Love Inspired Books, 195 Broadway, New York, NY 10007 U.S.A.

This is a work of fiction. Names, characters, places and incidents are either the product of the author's imagination or are used fictitiously, and any resemblance to actual persons, living or dead, business establishments, events or locales is entirely coincidental.

This edition published by arrangement with Love Inspired Books.

® and TM are trademarks of Love Inspired Books, used under license. Trademarks indicated with ® are registered in the United States Patent and Trademark Office, the Canadian Intellectual Property Office and in other countries.

www.Harlequin.com

Printed in U.S.A.

For all people will walk every one in the name of his god, and we will walk in the name of the Lord our God forever and ever.

—*Micah* 4:5

For Elizabeth McIntyre
Thanks for keeping us on track.
And herding writers is
definitely harder than herding cats…

Chapter One

Paradise Springs
Lancaster County, Pennsylvania

When the night sky opened and it started raining, Katie Kay Lapp stopped by the side of the road, covered her face with her hands and began to cry. The cold downpour was the final insult in a day that had begun badly and gotten worse with each passing hour. How had she gotten to this point? Months ago, she'd been the center of attention of young men at any gathering. They'd vied for time with her and for the chance to take her home in their courting buggies. Now she was abandoned and afraid and had no place to go.

You could go home.

Ach, it was easy for the little voice in her head—the one nagging her endlessly about doing the right thing—to say that. But she'd burned her bridges behind her and in front of her and around her. She couldn't go home. Her sisters would welcome her, but *Daed* would insist on knowing every detail of what she'd done since she ran away. He'd want to pray with her and ask her to repent for any sins she'd committed.

And she'd committed a bunch. Some intentionally and others by accident. In the eyes of Bishop Reuben Lapp, what she'd done would need to be repented for with prayer before it could be forgiven.

She moaned aloud when she imagined telling her *daed* about her fear that she was pregnant. Many plain women her age were married with one or more *bopplin*, but she hadn't been ready to settle down and lead an Amish life, the only life she'd ever known until she left home four months ago to find out what the rest of the world was like. It hadn't been a carefree *rumspringa* decision. Instead, she'd made the choice with care and a lot of deep consideration.

Or so she'd thought at the time.

Raindrops slid beneath her T-shirt and down her spine like a cascade of ice cubes. October could be a beautiful month in southeastern Pennsylvania or unforgiving like tonight.

Straightening, Katie Kay looked around. She wasn't sure where she was. Somewhere in rural Lancaster County, she knew, but not exactly where. She hadn't paid any attention. She'd been surprised when Austin, whom she'd described to others as her *Englisch* boyfriend because she'd foolishly believed he cared about her, had driven her and a couple of other *Englischers* out of Lancaster City, but she hadn't watched where they were going. Rain had been falling, and the streetlights had glittered on the windshield, disguising any landmarks in splattered light. She hadn't expected she'd need to know. She'd thought she was returning to the apartment she shared with Austin and their friends.

Not her friends, she knew. Neither had protested when Austin snatched her cell phone from her purse and ordered her out of the car. Maybe Vinnie and Juan, his

Englisch friends, had been as astounded as she'd been, never guessing he'd drive off and not come back for her.

She kept walking. She didn't have any other choice. The country road was two narrow lanes that curved and rose and fell over the rolling hillsides. It was edged on both sides by harvested fields. She peered through the darkness, but the lights she could see appeared to be a mile or two in the distance. Was she somewhere without many houses? Or were there ones between her and the distant lights? Amish houses wouldn't be lit this late in the evening because the people living in them usually rose before the sun and were in bed soon after sunset.

Two cars raced toward her. If the drivers saw her, they gave no sign, not swerving to the middle of the road to make sure they avoided her as they passed. The tires of the second sent a shower of dirty water over her.

"It's not fair!" she cried out. Nothing had been fair since her *mamm* died five years ago. Everyone had expected her to step into the role of housekeeper for her *daed.* After all, her half sister had when *Daed*'s first wife died. But Priscilla was the perfect Amish daughter and now was the perfect Amish wife and *mamm.* Katie Kay had been the one who questioned everything and was too curious to accept things just because someone told her so.

But look where curiosity had gotten her. A part of her wanted to pray, but she silenced that longing as she had for four months. Reaching out to God seemed like admitting she couldn't survive on her own among *Englischers.*

And why would God want to hear from her after she'd turned her back on Him and the life He'd given her? Another bridge she'd burned and wondered if it could ever be rebuilt.

A familiar sound came from behind her. Metal wheels on asphalt accompanied by iron horseshoes clip-clopping in a steady rhythm.

Katie Kay knew the source of those sounds. They'd been a part of her life since her earliest memories. Stepping off the edge of the road, she considered going down the slope toward a shadowed hedgerow until after the buggy had passed. An Amish person wouldn't go by her without stopping as the cars had, but she needed to avoid plain people until she figured out where she was.

Her feet refused to move. Her own body rebelled against standing a moment longer than necessary in the cold rain. Maybe she should try to hitch a ride with the buggy, so she could find shelter before the rain turned to sleet. Who would recognize her as the wayward daughter of Reuben Lapp, a beloved bishop?

The clatter of the wheels began to slow, and she knew she'd been seen in the lights connected to the buggy. Again, she was torn between running away and running toward it. How could she have gotten herself to this point? A few months ago, she'd been the pampered daughter of a respected Amish bishop. Now she was cowering by the side of a country road, left behind like a discarded kitten dropped by a heartless owner.

Which wasn't far off from the truth. Austin hadn't tossed her out of the car, but he'd raised his hand when she hesitated to follow his orders. Though he'd never struck her, she'd seen him flatten a man a head taller than him with a single blow. Again she told herself she shouldn't have been honest with him about her suspicion she might be pregnant until she was absolutely sure. Austin Moore prided himself on being a man without a single obligation to anyone or anything, and she should have known he'd refuse to take responsibility if she'd conceived. She wasn't sure, though signs pointed in that direction. By now, he'd be at the apartment in Lancaster they'd shared with two other *Englischers*, and he'd be watching sports and drinking whatever was in the fridge. He wouldn't spare her another thought. It wasn't as if he loved her.

And that realization was the most painful of all.

A voice called from the buggy that had pulled alongside her while the rain fell relentlessly on her bare head. "Katie Kay? Katie Kay Lapp, is it you?" Surprise lifted the deep voice several notches, but she recognized it.

Micah Stoltzfus!

Out of everyone in Lancaster County, why did *he* have to be in the buggy?

Micah had taken her home—several times—from social events, and she'd even let him kiss her. She'd decided she liked him well enough, and she'd enjoyed his kisses, but she wasn't interested in someone who kept talking about the future. She'd been happy focusing on the present, when there were a lot of *gut*-looking guys eager to take her home.

Why not enjoy what was going on and let tomorrow worry about itself?

That had been her motto, but now she was being forced to see where such a shortsighted plan had left her.

Alone.

Possibly pregnant.

And about to have to beg help from a man she'd told to get lost a year ago.

The petite woman standing beside his buggy bore little resemblance to the vivacious beauty he'd admired for years, but Micah Stoltzfus knew he wasn't mistaken. Though she didn't answer him and confirm her identity, he recognized Katie Kay Lapp's oval face and very large blue eyes. Her blond hair was no longer pulled back beneath a white organdy *kapp*. It'd been cropped short with bangs above her tawny brows and hung around her shoulders, weighed down by the rain. He guessed the strands which had been silken when they escaped her bun and brushed his face would, when dry, bounce with each step she took. Instead of a simple dress, she wore blue jeans and a black T-shirt that looked as if it'd been ruined before she'd stood outside in the storm.

He wanted to ask her where she'd been and what she'd been doing since she had left her *daed*'s house after a big argument. Reuben had been troubled about her vanishing, fearing what might happen to his naïve daughter. Katie Kay had left behind a message stating she was going to live with an *Englisch* friend. She hadn't said which one or where or when she might come home. The burden of not knowing had bent Reuben's shoulders, and Micah believed only his plans to marry Wanda Stoltzfus, Micah's *mamm*, and his strong faith had kept the bishop from being ground down completely. Reuben was a shadow of the vibrant man he'd once been.

Instead of asking the questions taunting him, Micah called through the open door on the driver's side of his buggy, "Don't you want to get out of the rain?"

She nodded, biting her lower lip.

For a moment, he wondered if he was wrong about her being Katie Kay Lapp. The Katie Kay he knew never had been abashed or quiet. Instead she'd had a quick retort and an easy laugh. This pale wraith might look like the woman he'd known, but where had her bright sparkle gone?

He was being silly. The woman was Katie Kay Lapp.

She was walking in the direction of Paradise Springs, where both her family and his lived.

"*Komm* in," he said as he reached across the buggy to open the passenger side door. He shut the one on his side while she hurried around the buggy. The rain was falling harder, and he didn't want to get soaked before he reached home. He would have been there by now if he and his business partner, Sean Donnelly, hadn't needed to meet with a new client tonight.

He hoped he and Sean would get the job installing solar panels for a new client. Otherwise, it would have been a waste of an evening and a slow, cold ride home. Sean's wife, Gemma, had asked Micah to stay at their house overnight, but he hadn't wanted his family to worry when he didn't return to the farm.

And Katie Kay would have been left to walk along the road connecting Paradise Springs and Ronks in the heart of Lancaster County. He hadn't seen another vehicle, other than a couple of cars driving at an unsafe speed along the twisting road. Certainly no buggies, because any person with sense would be inside on an inclement night.

When Katie Kay climbed in and slid the door closed, she sat as far from him as possible in the small buggy. Which wasn't very far. If they both put their hands on the seat between them, their fingers would overlap.

As they used to when he took her home after a singing.

That's over and done with, he reminded himself. She'd made it clear the last time he took her home in his courting buggy that if he disappeared from the face of the earth, she'd be fine. Instead, she had gone away, jumping the fence to live with *Englischers*.

She didn't look at him or speak, but in the glow from the buggy's lights, he saw she was shivering.

"Here." He stretched his arm behind the seat and pulled out a towel he kept among his tools. He used it when he washed up after a hot day of working on a roof while installing solar panels.

"Thanks." She hesitated as if she'd be upset her first word to him wasn't in *Deitsch*, the language of the plain people, and he'd order her out of the buggy. Before he could ask why she acted like a beaten pup, she added in not much more than a whisper, *"Danki."*

"Sounds like you've gotten used to talking to your *Englisch* friends."

"They aren't my friends," she snapped and then turned away to dry her dripping hair.

At last! A glimpse of the self-assured Katie Kay, though he wished he hadn't had to be irksome to get her to respond. When they'd first started walking out together, he'd admired that aspect of her. He'd thought then that she could be the special one for him. When she'd selected him from among her admirers, he'd believed it meant something. What a fool he'd been!

Taking the reins, he slapped them on Rascal's back. The horse was the same dark gray as the storm clouds overhead. Rascal stepped on the road. Micah didn't need to convince him to a faster pace. The buggy horse was eager to get home and dry.

Katie Kay didn't say anything as they drove through the night. From the corner of his eye, he saw her squeezing water out of her hair and into the towel. She never glanced in his direction. He might as well have been invisible.

He pulled on the left rein to turn Rascal onto the road to the Lapp farm. The horse resisted.

"Let's go, Rascal," Micah said past clenched teeth. He couldn't let his irritation with the woman beside him make him upset at the buggy horse. Rascal wanted to go right to reach his dry stable.

A damp hand settled on his left arm. He hated the tingle erupting out from where Katie Kay touched him. After a year, she had the same effect on him. He was a bigger fool than he'd thought.

"Go some other way," she ordered. "Any other way."

"This is the fastest way to your house."

"No! You can't take me home."

"Of course I'm taking you home." He frowned. "Where else did you think I was taking you?"

"I don't care. Anywhere else." Her voice broke, and her whisper was raw. "Just not home. Please, Micah. Don't take me home."

He didn't bother to hide his shock. What had happened to her? He'd never heard her beg anyone for anything.

"You need to go home, Katie Kay. Your family has been beside themselves with worry about you. I'm taking you home."

"No, you're not!" She grabbed the passenger side door. "If you think I won't jump out of this buggy, then you're wrong."

"Don't be silly. You could hurt yourself."

"I didn't before," he thought he heard her mutter, but before he could ask if he'd heard her correctly, she said, "If you're going to be like that, Micah, stop and let me out."

"I'm not leaving you out here in the middle of a stormy night."

"And you're not taking me home." Again her voice broke. "I'm not ready to face them. Not yet."

Hardening his heart to her was impossible. They'd known each other all their lives. He'd counted her among his *gut* friends before he'd fallen for her. Her *daed* was marrying his *mamm* in a month.

Was that why Katie Kay had returned? For the wedding? If so, Reuben and *Mamm* would be overjoyed to see her. But why didn't she want to relieve her *daed*'s fears? Too much didn't make sense.

"Micah," she said softly, "please take me somewhere else."

"Where?"

"I don't know."

"Do you have any money? One of the hotels out on Route 30 might not be completely booked on a weeknight."

She rolled her eyes. "I don't have enough to pay for a room." Opening her soaked purse that sat in a damp spot on the seat, she gasped.

"What's wrong?"

"He took my money! I thought he was just taking my cell phone."

Micah's hands tightened on the reins. "He? Were you robbed?"

"Not exactly."

If she was trying to be baffling tonight, she was succeeding. Maybe if he tried a different approach...

"Katie Kay, I don't want to have to lie to Reuben when he talks about wondering where you are."

"I'm not asking you to lie. I'm asking you not to say anything about seeing me."

"That's splitting hairs."

"Maybe it is." Again she looked away. "But I can't face my family right now."

It was the second time she'd said those words. He

wanted to ask why she intended to avoid her family, but she looked dejected and lost, so unlike the girl he'd known. He pushed aside his objections. The Bible taught that they were supposed to help one another. Yet it also was at the very heart of God's commandments that the duty to honor one's parents must never be set aside for any reason.

He drew in the horse and sat with his elbows on his knees as the buggy slowed to a stop by the side of the road. He knew what he should do. He should haul her at top speed to her family's house. But that might do more damage than *gut*. She obviously needed time to prepare herself before she spoke to Reuben. Letting her have a day or two wouldn't make a big difference, and granting her a favor might be the very thing that kept her from jumping the fence again. At least until after she and Reuben had a chance to meet. Not knowing where she was had been hardest on the bishop. If they could reconcile, perhaps it would smooth over the situation, even if she chose to leave again.

"All right," he said, hoping he wasn't making a complete mess of everything and praying both Reuben and God would understand. "I may know someone who can put you up for tonight."

"Not among the *Leit*. The news would reach my family before dawn."

That was true. The Amish didn't use phones or email except for business, but nothing stayed a secret long in their tight-knit community. Jokingly referred to as the Amish grapevine, gossip and rumors flew faster than anything in cyberspace.

"These people are *Englischers*." He glanced at her clothing. "I'm sure you're accustomed to folks who aren't Amish. I'll ask my friends Sean and Gemma Donnelly to let you stay with them tonight."

"*Danki*, Micah!" Her frown eased for the first time since she'd gotten into the buggy, and his heart did a crazy little flip as it always did when she smiled at him. But, this time, he ignored it. He wouldn't make the same mistake of thinking she cared for him as much as he'd cared for her. He wouldn't make that mistake ever again!

"Don't thank me yet. I'm not helping you unless you agree to do what I ask."

At his stern tone, her smile faltered.

Micah plunged forward with what he knew he had to get her to agree to do. "I will help you find a place for tonight and won't mention to anyone you're here, but only if you agree to speak with your *daed*. Not tonight," he added when she started to protest. "Within a week."

"That's too soon."

"Then tell me how long you need."

"I don't know."

"I told you what I think is long enough. Tell me what you think is long enough before you speak with Reuben." He couldn't relent on this, though he wasn't sure she'd honor any agreement. The Katie Kay he used to know would have, but the one sitting beside him was a stranger.

"A month."

He sat straighter. "What? A whole month? Why do you need a month?"

"You don't need to know why. I need time to be sure about things. A lot of things." She raised her face toward him, and he could see the glitter in her eyes. Determination to get her way or tears or both? "If you'll find me a place to stay, Micah, I'll talk to my *daed* before a month's gone by. Agreed?"

He considered her words. If he said no, that wouldn't change anything. She wasn't going to talk to her *daed*. If he said *ja*, there was a chance she might do as she said. He owed Reuben that much.

Turning the horse's head back in the direction they'd come, he said, "Agreed."

She thanked him, but he paid no attention as he stared out into the darkness. He'd made the best decision he could have under the circumstances or the worst. He wasn't sure which.

Chapter Two

Micah assured Katie Kay while they drove through the darkness that his friends would be willing to take her in for the night. As to what she'd do tomorrow night, she wasn't sure. Maybe one of her *Englisch* friends would let her stay at her house. She must have one who wasn't afraid of Austin.

But most of her *Englisch* friends had been Austin's friends a lot longer than they'd been hers.

She'd never felt more alone. Her whole life, she'd been surrounded by friends, both female and male. As she grew up, the male friends became admirers, and she'd had fun flirting with them. Soon, if her suspicions that she was pregnant were true, none of them would be interested in her.

Though she'd glowered at Micah, he hadn't backed away from his insistence she speak with her *daed*. He'd always been stubborn, but she'd usually persuaded him to change his mind. Not tonight. She recognized the set of his square jaw, identical to his twin brother's, except Micah didn't have a cleft in his chin. His black hair fell into his startlingly blue eyes that saw so much and revealed so little. His days spent in construction work

had broadened his shoulders and knotted muscles in his
arms beneath his work coat. She couldn't believe some
girl hadn't snagged him as her husband in the past year.

And you should be glad for that. She hated listening to her conscience, but she couldn't argue with it. If
he hadn't been out tonight, she wasn't sure where she
could have found shelter without resorting to knocking on doors.

But Micah couldn't understand why she didn't want
to talk to her *daed* and she couldn't tell him the truth.
She needed to know if she was pregnant or not. And if
she was… With a sigh, she admitted she didn't know
what she'd do.

The house where Sean and Gemma Donnelly lived
was closer to Ronks than Paradise Springs. Katie Kay
was relieved because the two districts her *daed* oversaw
as a bishop didn't reach that far west. The Donnellys'
single-story house was close to the road, and, unlike
the plain houses they'd passed, bright lights glowed in
the windows. Electric wires ran high over the driveway, where a pair of vans, one with lettering on the
side, were parked. She couldn't read what was painted
on it, and she didn't care.

All she wanted was to have a place to sleep and to
wake in the morning to find tonight had been nothing but a nightmare. It had to be. Austin wouldn't have
treated her heartlessly, and her heroic knight in a gray
buggy wouldn't have been Micah. What a joke on her!

Drawing in his horse, Micah stopped the buggy next
to one van. She saw a hitching post nearby and wondered why it was there. Maybe the people inside pro-
vided a service to the plain community. He lashed the
reins around it while she stepped out with the towel
over her head to hold off the rain.

"This way," Micah said, walking along flagstones to the front door.

She followed without saying anything. When he knocked a couple of times and then opened the door, she knew he must be a regular visitor. Amish people walked in without knocking but not the *Englischers* she'd met. They'd been horrified the first time she entered without waiting for someone to open the door. She'd been mortified, not realizing then how many more mistakes she had ahead of her.

"Is something wrong, Micah?" asked an *Englischer* as he entered the narrow hallway on the other side of the door. He wasn't as tall as Micah, but he wore similar work clothes. His hair was red and tightly curled both on his head and in his thick beard and mustache.

"We didn't expect you back tonight." A woman followed the man into the hallway. She was plump and wore her dark hair in a ponytail. Dressed in a flowery bathrobe and fluffy slippers, she looked ready for bed. "Are you okay? Is Rascal all right?"

"We're fine. I left him tied out by the driveway," Micah answered, and Katie Kay realized Rascal must be his horse. An odd name for a buggy horse, but maybe the beast wasn't plodding and slow when the weather was *gut*. "Sean and Gemma Donnelly, this is my... friend. Katie Kay Lapp."

Did the others hear his hesitation? It made her sad, though she wasn't quite sure why. She'd treated him poorly, so she should be grateful he attached the word *friend* to her name. She needed a friend.

"Come inside," Gemma said with a welcoming smile. "What a horrible night to be out! Can I get you something hot to drink? I think there's cocoa left in the cupboard."

"Perfect," Katie Kay said at the same time Micah replied, "No, thanks, we don't need anything."

He frowned at her, and she wanted to ask why. Gemma had offered, and she'd accepted. She understood when Gemma turned, revealing the unmistakable outline of a very pregnant body. In a few months, she could look the same. Her fingers went to her belly. Was it as flat as it'd been a few weeks ago?

"Actually," Katie Kay hurried to add, "I'm fine. Being inside and warm is helping. I'll skip the cocoa." She hoped her stomach wouldn't growl and betray the fact she hadn't had anything to eat since noon, when she'd finally been able to hold down food. All morning, she'd been sick…as she had for the past week. She'd had to accept the possibility she was pregnant.

"Are you sure you don't want anything?" the woman asked.

"Ja." The *Deitsch* word slipped out as it hadn't in months. She was exhausted. That had to be the reason. It couldn't have anything to do with the brooding man beside her.

Such a description of Micah astonished her. Micah usually had been the one getting everyone to laugh. He and his brothers always teased each other, and if they could draw others into their sport, all the better. Yet, he stood like a disapproving Old Testament patriarch, not a hint of humor on his face.

The red-haired man asked, "What's up, Micah?"

"Katie Kay needs a place to stay tonight. Can she stay here with you?"

Questions flickered across both *Englischers*' faces, but she was relieved when, after a glance was exchanged, Gemma said, "Certainly. There's an extra bed in Olivia's room." She smiled at Katie Kay. "Olivia is our four-year-old daughter. I don't think she'd mind sharing her room as long as you're okay with sleeping with a chatterbox. She talks all day, as well as half the night in her sleep."

"That will be fine." What else could she say? She'd rather sleep in the rain? No, she was glad for the chance to be under a roof and warm. It hadn't been warm the past week in the apartment she shared with Austin and his friends. There hadn't been money to pay for heat, so they'd used what blankets they had and hoped the winter wouldn't be bad. "Is Olivia your only child?"

She ignored the look Micah fired at her when she didn't use the common *Deitsch* word for child. Why would she say *kind*? The Donnellys weren't Amish, and she had no idea how much of the language they understood. Probably some, because they were Micah's friends.

"No," Gemma replied with another warm smile. "We have two sons. DJ, which is short for Sean Donnelly Junior, is going to turn six in January, and Jayden is almost two." She laced her hands together over her distended belly. "And this is son number three. Dylan. He'll be here in a couple of months. His due date is Christmas, but he'll come when he wants. As they all do." She laughed, but a hint of fatigue slipped in. "Sean, why don't you help Micah get her bags?"

"I don't have any," she said.

"Oh." Gemma regained her composure. "Well, then we won't have to worry about Sean clomping up the stairs and waking the kids. Come in and sit down. We just finished watching the news."

As they walked into a comfortable living room with bright green-and-white wallpaper on one wall and a fireplace on another, Micah glanced at Katie Kay, this time with an expectant expression. What did he want? *Ach*, he wanted her to thank his friends, and he believed she'd left her manners behind in Lancaster. As she started to express her gratitude to Gemma, feeling the familiar ripples of rebellion rising at his silent chiding, her hostess waved aside her words.

"We're more than happy to help any friend of Micah's," the woman said but glanced at him with an unsteady smile.

No doubt, Gemma wondered what Micah, so Amish with his broadfall pants and straw hat, was doing with a woman who wasn't wearing plain clothes and who had no luggage other than a drenched purse.

"We appreciate that," Micah said, saving her from having to explain. "When I come in the morning, we'll figure out what she'll do next. Okay, Katie Kay?"

Regarding her without a speck of emotion, he held her gaze. She might as well have been a plank of wood or a shingle. A shiver ran along her as she wondered if he despised her as much as he acted. Tears clogged her throat. She was more alone than she'd ever been.

She looked away first. She didn't want him to see her eyes fill. She wasn't going to cry as she had out on the road. Somehow she had to be strong. If not for herself, then for the *boppli* she might be carrying.

Though Katie Kay hadn't replied to Micah's question, everyone acted as if she had. Micah took his leave, and Gemma showed her to her daughter's room. Her hostess explained that Micah and her husband owned a company together, so Micah came over every morning to catch a ride with Sean to work.

Trying to act as if she'd been in a house like this many times before, she knew the *Englisch* habits she'd tried to adopt still looked unnatural on her because

Gemma asked if she was familiar with how to switch on electric lights in the nearby bathroom. Austin had teased her about being too "dumb-dumb Dutch"—his derogatory term for plain people—each time she made a mistake. She had tried to appear sophisticated and *Englisch* in the hope he'd notice her.

He had one night, the one she didn't recall much about. The result of it was the reason he'd thrown her out of his car and his life.

Why didn't she remember more of what had happened a couple of months ago? She'd been drinking, as she often did with the roommates, but she usually was careful, never having more than one drink because even that could make her head swim. The others would have can after can of beer until they passed out. She hadn't. Having finally gained a little control over her life, she didn't want to chance losing it again.

But one night she hadn't been cautious because she wanted to forget the bad day she'd had at work waiting tables at a diner. Nothing she'd done had been right, and when she got back to the apartment, she'd given into Austin's urging to keep drinking. Now she was paying the price for believing he wanted to comfort her. She couldn't blame him for her stupidity, but she did for his callous expulsion of her from his life.

Taking the nightgown Gemma loaned her as well as a toothbrush, she skipped the hot shower she wanted desperately. The Donnellys were ready to call it a day, and she didn't want to keep them up. She thanked Gemma, slipped into the little girl's room and got ready for bed.

It was far softer than any bed she'd slept on since leaving her own comfortable bed at home. Instead of a handmade quilt, the blanket and freshly laundered sheets were covered by an afghan. Its extra warmth would be welcome.

From the other bed, Olivia mumbled something. Katie Kay moved to check the *kind* and bumped into the table between the beds. Something fell off it and bounced on the floor. She realized it was an inhaler. She looked from it to the *kind*. Olivia must have asthma.

She put the device on the table and moved to Olivia's bed. In the faint light from a night-light shaped like a princess, the little girl's curly hair looked dark, but Katie Kay guessed it was as red as her *daed*'s. Her cheeks were as full as a well-fed squirrel's, and she clutched a well-worn, well-loved stuffed kitten to her pajamas that were decorated with more princesses.

Another flurry of tears threatened to fall as Katie Kay smoothed the covers over the sleeping *kind*. Olivia didn't resemble Sarann, but Katie Kay remembered tucking in her youngest sister before getting into her own bed. Sarann hadn't lived to be any older than this little girl; yet that had been far longer than any *kind* with her birth defects should have lived. Every day of her life, she'd had a smile in spite of the pain she must have suffered.

If Katie Kay had been half as courageous, maybe she wouldn't have taken the easy way out and left Paradise Springs. *Daed* had been patient and loving with Sarann, seeing her as a special gift from God. No different from any of his *kinder*, as he'd said on many occasions.

Why was she remembering that now? She'd let her anger at him banish the memory. Well, it was too late to change anything, and she couldn't return home. Not when she was unsure if she was pregnant. Not when she hadn't made up her mind about being baptized and becoming a member of the Amish community. Not when she was confused about so many things.

Including Micah Stoltzfus. She'd changed a lot in the past four months, but she hadn't expected him to be different, as well. How many times had she joked that nothing ever changed among the plain people?

Something else to add to the long list of things she'd been wrong about.

Going to the other bed, Katie Kay slipped under the covers. Her hair was damp and fell against her face as she turned her head on the pillow to stare out the window at the rain.

In the morning, Micah would be back. She needed to make a plan for what she was going to do.

She wished she knew what that might be.

Guarding every word he spoke the next morning was almost more than Micah could handle. He sat at the breakfast table with his married brother, Ezra, and Ezra's wife, Leah, and her young niece, as well as *Mamm* and his other unmarried brothers. His twin, Daniel, and their older brother Isaiah both were getting married later in the fall. Daniel had built a house beyond the barn where his fiancée already lived, and Isaiah spent most of his time down the road with his late friend's family that had become his own.

Nobody had spoken of anything connected to Katie Kay. Even so, he couldn't think of anything other than the blonde who'd returned to Paradise Springs after living somewhere with the *Englisch* for almost four months.

Only four months? From the lines dug into Reuben's face by his unrelenting worry, the bishop looked, when Micah had last seen him on Sunday, as if Katie Kay had left years ago. But it'd been June when she left, and now it was October.

He shouldn't have told Katie Kay he'd say nothing to anyone about her return. That was wrong, and he intended to tell her so as soon as he saw her at the Donnellys' house this morning. But what if she reneged on her side of the bargain, too, and left without ever seeing Reuben? How could Micah face his bishop knowing he could have taken Katie Kay—willing or not—to her *daed* last night?

He'd get to the Donnellys' house early. Sean wasn't a morning person, something Micah had learned since the two of them had become partners about three months ago. Daniel, Micah's twin, had invited him to join Stoltzfus Brothers Construction, the company Daniel had started earlier in the year. However, for a couple of years, Micah and Sean had been talking about working together every time they were at the same construction site. They'd pooled their savings and started Plain and Simple Solutions, an alternative energy company.

"You're plain, and I'm simple," Sean had said with a laugh when he suggested the name.

"I've noticed that," he'd replied with a chuckle of his own. Sean was anything but simple. He was a brilliant carpenter and a great salesman, finding client after client, so they never were idle. However, the name was perfect for what they did. Simple, green solutions to help *Englischers* cut their power bills and to enable plain households to get electricity that didn't come from the grid.

One after another, his brothers prayed silently before they rose from the table and went to their various jobs. Leah and her niece disappeared down cellar, probably to get canned vegetables and meat for the evening meal.

Micah barely noticed them leaving as he wondered if Katie Kay would keep her side of the bargain, even if he'd kept his. He wished he could trust her, but he couldn't.

For the past year, his brothers had teased him for not asking if he could take her home. They believed he was too shy to talk to her. None of them had any idea of the truth. He'd asked her, driven her home several times and then she'd told him to go bother some other girl and waved him away as if he were as annoying as a gnat.

He had collected the pieces of his broken heart and prayed God would help her see she'd made a mistake. If God had, she hadn't listened to Him. Last weekend, he'd taken Isaiah's late wife's sister Tillie Mast, home from a youth event…to get his brothers off his back. She was sweet and well-known as a great cook. He'd learned, however, contrary to the old adage, that the way to his heart was not through his stomach. He doubted he was giving her a chance, but he'd promised himself he wouldn't make a fool of himself over a woman again.

"Micah?"

He looked up from his scrambled eggs and fried potatoes when *Mamm* said his name in a tone that suggested she'd already repeated it more than once. *"Ja?"*

"Is there someone special you'd like to sit with at the wedding supper?"

The old tradition of pairing off the singles for the evening meal to give them a chance to get to know each other better was one he wished *Mamm* and Reuben would skip. Forcing a smile, he said, "No one in particular."

"Not Tillie Mast?"

"You'd do her a big favor by matching her with someone else." He wasn't surprised his *mamm* knew about him taking Tillie home. Eager eyes at the end of an evening noted who left with whom. Because he and Katie Kay had been careful, at her insistence, nobody had noticed them together.

"I'm sorry to hear that, Micah." She patted his cheek. "You're a *gut* boy, and you deserve someone special in your life."

"I trust God will send her along eventually."

Mamm picked up her empty cup and carried it to the stove to refill it with *kaffi*. Holding the cup to let the fragrant steam rise into her face, she said, "Reuben had hoped you and Katie Kay might sit together."

"What?" He sat straighter and berated himself for not leaving at the same time as his brothers had.

"I hear how Daniel teases you, and I've learned there's a nugget of truth in the jests you two throw at each other." She took a sip and lowered her cup. "*Ach*, it's impossible anyhow, but I keep hoping that girl will come to her senses and return home. It would mean the world to Reuben."

"I know." Guilt stabbed him. As soon as he reached Sean's house, he was going to get Katie Kay and drive her home, whether she agreed or not. He didn't want to be caught in the middle of this mess any longer.

"Do you know where she might be, Micah?" His *mamm* went on as he tried not to choke out the truth. "Listen to me. Why would you know where she is? Though the two of you were *gut* friends when you were younger, things changed." Sorrow dimmed her eyes. "If you know someone who might know where she is, pass the word along that she is missed."

"I will." He intended to tell Katie Kay himself. Bowing his head and saying words of gratitude for the meal while he hoped the Lord would forgive him for his haste, he got up, gave his *mamm* a hug and hurried out before she could say more.

By the time he had Rascal hitched to his buggy and was on his way to the Donnellys' house, the sun was turning the eastern sky from black to layers of gray clouds. He practiced over and over what he'd say to Katie Kay. Last night, asking her to be sensible hadn't worked. In fact, he'd probably insulted her by suggesting she wasn't acting rationally.

"She isn't," he mumbled to himself as he turned onto the road leading toward Ronks. "Why would she return if she didn't intend to mend the fences she's jumped over?"

He was missing something important, but what?

The Donnellys' house was dark except for a light in the kitchen. Micah parked his buggy behind the lime-green antique Volkswagen van that Gemma drove. He stepped out and around the more modern van Sean had painted with their company's name and phone number, which Gemma answered in the house. Having her help had been a big step toward getting the company going, but Micah wondered if they should hire an answering service. Gemma would be overwhelmed with three young *kinder*, a *boppli* and handling the calls. He'd have to talk to Sean about it. His friend was hesitant to make changes that didn't have an impact on Micah, too. For once, Sean needed to be a bit selfish and think of himself and his family.

Especially after Micah had selfishly left his problem with Sean and Gemma last night. While Gemma had settled Katie Kay, Micah had given his partner an overview of the situation and realized how little he knew about what had brought Katie Kay to Paradise Springs. He planned to get answers today.

"Come in, Micah," said Gemma, meeting him at the door.

She didn't usually do that, so he asked, "Is everything okay? Has Katie Kay been—?"

"Sit down, Micah."

"What's wrong?" He couldn't miss the underlying tension in her voice. He'd been about to ask what Katie Kay had done to upset the household, but he restrained himself. Bringing her to the Donnellys' house had been wrong. He'd transferred his problem to his best friends.

"You should sit down, Micah."

"Just tell me." How much trouble had Katie Kay caused?

Gemma took a deep breath and then let it out with a sigh. "I think your friend is pregnant."

"Pregnant?" He groped for a chair and sat as he stared at her. "That can't be true!"

"Because her father is a bishop?" She shook her head with a grimace. "Don't fool yourself, Micah. Her running away was already aimed at hurting him and tossing aside everything she'd been taught. Getting involved with some man wasn't much of a step further."

He couldn't help thinking of Katie Kay saying someone had taken her money along with her cell phone. Was it the man who was the *daed* of her *boppli*? He felt his temper rise but pushed it down. Getting angry wouldn't solve anything. In fact, it might make things worse.

"Where is she?" he asked, relieved his voice sounded close to normal.

"Throwing up." She looked behind her as Sean came into the kitchen.

For once, his friend wasn't complaining about the early hour and how work should begin at noon. Instead, he looked from his wife to Micah and sighed. "I guess it's obvious why she didn't want to go home. What do you want to do?"

"I want you two to go to work," Gemma said before he could answer. "I've got an unused pregnancy test kit. I'll take care of her today. You take time to think about what you want to say, Micah." She gave him a sad smile. "I know you two used to date."

"I took her home a few times."

"Which is dating among the Amish." She wagged a finger at him as if he were as young as her *kinder.* "Don't try to pull the wool over my eyes."

"You sound like *Mamm.*"

"And you sound like you're trying to change the subject." Her *gut* humor fell away as she added, "Katie Kay needs to confirm if she's pregnant or not before she has to face anyone, including you." She sighed. "Maybe especially you. I can see she respects you a great deal."

He snorted his disagreement.

Gemma frowned. "Stop acting like a sulking teenager and listen to me. She's a young woman in a bad situation. She doesn't have anyone she can turn to."

"The *boppli*'s *daed* can—"

"I don't think he's in the picture any longer. She hasn't said, though she opened up to me a bit more this morning. Or maybe she slipped up and spoke without thinking. She mentioned something about him chucking her out of his car last night like litter."

The curses the other construction workers used raced through Micah's head. He pushed them away and sent an apology to God, but the *gut* Lord surely understood.

How could a man get a woman with *kind* and then abandon her in an icy rain?

Gemma put comforting fingers on his arm, but it wasn't any solace when he recalled how Katie Kay's same motion had sent ripples of sensation coursing through him. Why did he have feelings for her? He didn't want to get enmeshed in her charms again. His heart didn't need to be broken once more.

"I know what you're thinking, Micah," she said, "because I feel the same way. Any good Christian would. However, we must deal with what *is*, not what we would like it to be."

The sound of *kinder* came from upstairs. Gemma motioned for him and Sean to go and kissed her husband before hurrying to collect the youngsters.

Sean opened the door so Micah could lead the way out. When his friend didn't ask any questions, Micah was grateful. Everything was changing. Gemma was right. He needed to take time to think because he was less sure now about what he should do than he had been the night before.

Chapter Three

Concentrating on work wasn't easy, and more than once during the day, Micah was glad he wore the safety rope that kept him from tumbling off the roof. He wasn't watching where he was stepping. He was also grateful he and Sean and the two men they'd hired to assist them were preparing the support framework to hold the panels being installed on the newly constructed house. With his mind elsewhere, he didn't want to be responsible for carrying the expensive twenty-five-pound panels up the ladder and setting them in place.

The end of the workday arrived, and Micah came to the realization his plans hadn't changed from that morning. He needed to talk to Katie Kay and insist she decide. She had to make up her mind and go home or go away.

But if she chose the latter, how would he ever explain to Reuben that he'd abetted Katie Kay? He prayed God would give him the words. She'd been too distraught last night to make a *gut* decision. But now she'd had a day to think about her future.

Micah stowed his tools in the rear of the van and got in on the passenger side. Sean was already behind the wheel. Reaching for the key, he started the engine as Micah hooked his seat belt in place.

Neither of them spoke as they left the subdivision that soon would consist of nearly twenty new houses. Each would have solar panels, so he and Sean had several weeks of work ahead of them.

"How are you doing?" Sean asked, breaking the silence.

"If I knew, I'd tell you."

His friend gave him a sympathetic grin. "You'll feel better after you get this conversation with Katie Kay over with."

"I hope so." He didn't mean to give terse answers, but he wasn't sure what else to say.

Sean glanced at him and then back at the road. "I think it'd be a good idea if I get Gemma and the kids out of the way so you can talk to Katie Kay without us."

"Sean—"

"I promised them I'd take them out to a restaurant across from the Rockvale Outlets. It might as well be tonight."

"You're a *gut* friend."

"And you're a good partner. If you fall and break your neck because you aren't paying attention to the job, I'll have to find and train another." He looked away from the road again and gave Micah a brash grin. "I know how long that takes because, after all this time, I've barely got you trained."

Micah appreciated his friend's attempt to tease him out of his somber mood, so, though he didn't feel the least bit like laughing, he did. "I think you've got it backward. *I* have been training you. You didn't know which end of the panel went where when I first met you."

"Yeah, yeah. Keep telling yourself that if it gives you comfort."

He listened as Sean continued jesting and tried to laugh at the appropriate times. The truth was, however, that nothing could make him feel better about talking with Katie Kay. No matter what the results of the pregnancy test had been, there still was the issue of her refusal to see her family.

When Sean pulled the van into the driveway, Micah tried to breathe slowly. This wasn't going to be easy, but he had to convince Katie Kay to do what she should and go home. If she was pregnant, she needed her family more than ever.

Micah gave his friend a brief smile when Sean clapped him on the shoulder as they walked to the front door. As always, Micah let Sean open the door. As always, a whirl of *kinder*, looking more like a dozen than three, surrounded Sean. Their young voices told him about their day at the same time, each trying to talk over the other. No matter how many times Gemma or Sean urged them to take turns, they were too excited to have their *daed* home at day's end.

Standing aside to let the loving assault run its course, Micah couldn't help envying his partner. Having a house filled with cute *kinder* and a loving wife who somehow found a way to stand on tiptoe and kiss him over the heads of the excited youngsters would be a true blessing. After seeing his siblings marry and begin to raise families, he'd known it was something he wanted for himself.

As if he'd spoken out loud, the *kinder* threw their arms around him next, spewing out more of the stories they'd started telling their *daed*. To them, he was Uncle Micah, though two-year-old Jayden could manage only Mike. He hugged each one in turn, not wanting his anxiety to ruin their happiness.

The kids cheered when Sean announced they were eating out. Gemma smiled, too, but hers was as taut as Micah's felt. When she glanced at him, she didn't say anything. It wasn't necessary. He could tell from her strained expression that the pregnancy test had been positive.

He helped get the *kinder* into their coats and hats. When he offered to help put them in their seats in the car, Sean shook his head.

"We'll take care of them. You take care of her." He gripped Micah's arm and then herded his wife and *kinder* out the door.

Micah closed it. Once he heard the car back out of the drive, he went into the living room. Where was Katie Kay?

As if in answer, he heard dishes rattling in the kitchen. He went in.

Katie Kay wore the same jeans, but they'd been washed. Her battered T-shirt had been replaced by a black sweater. It brought out the gold in her hair, which she pulled back with clips that must have belonged to Olivia. One was topped by a red dog and the other a blue cat that was the exact same shade as Katie Kay's eyes. She had only socks on, and he wondered if her shoes had been ruined in the rain.

"Oh, it's you," she said as she closed the cupboard door.

"Hello to you, too." He put his straw hat on the island and undid his stained work coat. "Sean is taking the family out for supper. A treat for the *kinder*."

"Gemma said he might." Her voice was as unemotional as his. "She told me there are leftovers in the fridge and to help myself. Do you want something before you go?"

"I want to talk to you."

Her eyes narrowed with suspicion. He'd known he couldn't fool her with casual conversation. "What about?"

"You."

"I don't want to hear how disappointed you are in me or how you believe I should go to my family's house." She reached into the refrigerator and pulled out a plastic container with a bright green top. "You've made yourself clear on that."

"*Gut*, then we can talk about something else. Do you want to talk about you being pregnant?"

Color washed from her face, and the container fell out of her fingers to bounce on the kitchen floor. She grabbed the edge of the counter as he picked up the plastic box and set it beside his hat. Red sauce was leaking out. He pulled a section of paper towel off the roll by the sink and stuck it under the container. He wanted to give her a chance to find her voice, so it wouldn't feel like he was interrogating her.

"You know about that?" she asked.

"This morning, Gemma told me what she suspected. She's worried about you."

"About you, you mean." She crossed her arms in front of herself in a protective pose.

"You know Sean and Gemma are my friends. Of course they're concerned about me, but she's worried about you, too. She's that way."

Katie Kay's shoulders lost their rigid stance. "You're right. She cares a lot, though I'm a stranger."

"You're someone who needs help. That's all she and Sean have to know. They're usually among the first to help anyone in the community, whether the person is plain or *Englisch*." He gave her a wry half smile. "She told me this morning because she wanted me to help you, too."

"This morning, I didn't know for sure." As fast as her face had bleached, it reddened.

"But you used the pregnancy test and found out you are."

"Do you know all my secrets?" she cried, flinging her hands in the air and storming past him. "I thought I could trust Gemma to keep her mouth zipped."

For a moment, she acted as if she intended to stamp out of the kitchen, and he was prepared to give chase because they couldn't postpone this conversation, especially since a *boppli* had been added to the mix. When she turned and faced him, he hid his surprise. In the past, Katie Kay had run away from whatever bothered her. Tonight, she held her ground. Another sign she'd changed.

But for the better or the worse?

"Gemma didn't say anything," he assured her. "I could tell by how worried she looked." He looked her steadily in the eyes. "I am concerned, too."

"I don't need you worrying about me. I got myself into this situation. I'll deal with it myself."

"How?" he fired back, his frustration escaping.

She froze at his sharp question, and, for one moment, it was as if she were a balloon and his words a pin cutting into her. She deflated, and he crossed the room and took her arm before her knees folded beneath her. By the time she tried to pull it away, he'd sat her at the table.

He leaned one hand beside her and caught her gaze again. He was awed by the intensity of the pain and fear in her eyes, but he saw her resolve, too. As he watched, a quiet strength submerged the despair.

"How?" he asked. "How are you going to deal with this by yourself, Katie Kay?"

That *was* the question, Katie Kay admitted. Trust Micah to get to the heart of the matter. Her *daed* admired his frankness, which Micah had inherited from his own *daed*. It was a *gut* question, and she wished she had an answer. She and Gemma had talked most of the day when they weren't entertaining the *kinder*. DJ went to kindergarten in the morning, and the numbness left by the results of the pregnancy test had started to wear off for Katie Kay by the time the youngster got home.

"Your family will want to help you," Micah said.

Raising her eyes to his deeper blue ones, she could see he believed what he said. Most likely, he was right, but if she went home, everyone would expect her to fit into the constraints of an Amish woman's life. Gemma Donnelly had shown her *Englischers* could be as giving and compassionate as a plain person. Katie Kay had started doubting that when she went to live with Austin and his friends after her nearby *Englisch* friend's parents made it obvious she'd worn out her welcome. They'd been fine with her visiting, but they had Amish friends they hadn't wanted to upset by letting her stay longer.

"It's not that, Micah."

"Then what is it?"

How could she explain to a man who'd already been baptized and joined the Amish community? Micah always had an eye on the future, making plans for what he hoped to do. Her *daed* had mentioned it to her, probably in hopes of convincing her to do the same. But taking such an irrevocable step meant turning away from the wider world.

She wasn't like Micah. She wasn't focused on what could happen tomorrow. She wanted to savor today and the exciting things it might contain. What if she did get baptized and there were amazing things in the *Englisch* world she never had a chance to experience? She didn't want to miss out.

Austin and his friends had a word for it. *FOMO*. Fear of missing out. It described her feelings, but, when she looked at Micah's handsome face—and he'd gotten better-looking in the past year—she doubted he'd understand. Somehow, he'd found a way to strike a balance between the plain and *Englisch* worlds. She was still trying to find her way.

"I have to think of the *boppli*," she said, selecting the easiest excuse she could devise. "When I see this family, I know I want that for him or her."

"The *boppli*'s *daed*—"

"Isn't it pretty obvious he doesn't want anything to do with either of us?" She hated the bitterness in her voice, but how could she have misjudged Austin so completely?

"I'm sorry, Katie Kay."

His sympathy almost undid her. She wasn't going to cry again. Austin wasn't worth her tears. If she'd seen that right from the beginning, instead of thinking he was much cooler than the guys she'd grown up with because he had a car and an apartment, she wouldn't be in the situation she was in. She couldn't change the past, but it was time to stand up for herself.

"Danki." She gave him the best smile she could manage.

"What can I do to help?"

She shook her head. "I don't think there's anything you can do. Gemma has invited me to stay as long as I need to."

"I didn't realize that." His tone made it clear he wasn't happy with his business partner's wife making the offer.

"You didn't think she'd toss me out, too, did you?"

"No. I know Gemma too well."

"But you don't want me to take advantage of your friends, ain't so?" The Amish phrase fell from her lips as easily as if she'd never been away.

"I didn't say that."

"You didn't have to." She stood. "Your opinion is splashed all over your face. Micah, I don't need your help. There's nothing you can do to help me."

"I can marry you."

Katie Kay stared at him in disbelief. He couldn't have said what she thought he'd said. Not after what she'd done, both in Paradise Springs and after she left. He knew too many of her faults, and if he'd ever cared about her, she'd squashed any hint of love by telling him to get out of her life.

He must have forgiven her, because he was trying to help her. But that, she knew, was the Amish way. Forgive others for their mistakes and move ahead as if the transgression had never happened. She'd never managed to make it work herself, though she'd tried over and over.

When she didn't reply, Micah folded his arms over his chest and looked at her with a glacial expression she found impossible to decipher. "You should know one thing before you answer, Katie Kay. I didn't offer to marry you because of feelings I have for you."

"Y-y-you d-d-didn't?" she sputtered, shocked.

"No." He picked up his hat from the counter. "I offered because I admire your *daed*, and I don't want to see him and *Mamm* hurt."

"What does Wanda have to do with this?" She considered Micah's *mamm* a bit of a *buttinsky*—a word she'd learned from Austin's friends—and an inveterate matchmaker.

He stared at her, and emotion returned to his face. It was disbelief. "You really don't know?"

"Know what?"

"Your *daed* and my *mamm* are getting married next month."

Katie Kay sat again, so hard the chair rocked. She tried to wrap her mind around the idea *Daed* was marrying Wanda Stoltzfus. They'd been *gut* friends for years. Wanda often sent a *snitz* pie home with *Daed* when he went to the Stoltzfus farm for one reason or another. Apparently he'd really had only a single reason for going to visit. He'd been courting Micah's *mamm*.

"I can't believe it," she whispered.

"They decided after you left. Reuben has been praying you'd return for the ceremony, so all his *kinder* will be there."

She looked at her flat abdomen. "I'm not sure he'll want me there."

"If you apologize to him and are married—"

"I'm not marrying you, Micah Stoltzfus! Didn't I make that clear last year?"

"You did." He put on his straw hat and buttoned his coat. "And don't worry. I won't bother you by asking you again. You've made yourself clear tonight. *Guten owed*, Katie Kay." Without another word, he walked out of the kitchen. Seconds later, she heard the front door open and close.

She didn't move as the sound of buggy wheels rolling after a horse faded into the night. She'd handled it wrong. She should have thanked Micah for his offer before she turned him down. He'd been candid when he told her that he was asking her to protect their parents from pain.

Maybe you should have considered his offer. He might not have feelings for you, but you have plenty for him.

"Shut up!" She jumped to her feet and ran into the living room. Turning on the television, she kept pushing the volume button on the remote until the sound of voices and laughter were so loud her ears hurt. But it was useless. Nothing drowned out the truth. She may have lost her best ally as she faced the future alone.

Chapter Four

Slowly Katie Kay sank to sit on the Donnellys' front-porch step. She'd come outside after the family had returned home. She didn't want to ruin their excitement after their fun evening out, and she was too distressed to try to pretend she was all right.

The chilly evening wind was overwhelmed by the cold sinking deep within her as Micah's words replayed through her mind. *Daed* was getting remarried? Why hadn't someone told her? She wasn't under the *bann*. She hadn't been baptized yet, something she'd avoided discussing each time her *daed* had brought up the subject, so leaving wasn't a reason to shun her. Why hadn't one of her sisters let her know about this astonishing event?

Maybe because she hadn't written to any of them after she left Paradise Springs and moved to Lancaster. They wouldn't have known how to reach her.

She hid her face in her hands. While she'd been gone, it'd been easy to convince herself nothing would change here. Wasn't that one of the reasons she'd gone? Because everything stayed the same day after day while the outside, *Englisch* world buzzed by at warp speed?

But she was back. If she was in Paradise Springs when the wedding was held, should she attend? Her hand slipped over her abdomen. It was flat. With the right dress, she shouldn't have to reveal the truth in a month. She could go and see her friends and enjoy a bit of flirting and...

Those days were over. She'd put an end to them when she left Paradise Springs and sought the brighter lights and faster pace of Lancaster City.

And Micah knew the truth. He wouldn't spread it, but it would be only a matter of time before someone else discovered she hadn't come home alone.

Again she wanted to ask God why He had arranged for Micah to be the person whose path crossed hers. Was she being punished for being headstrong and curious about the *Englischers*? Hadn't *Daed* taught that their Heavenly Father forgave each of them as He asked them to forgive each other?

The cold air finally drove her inside. She was relieved to discover the family had gone to bed, but loneliness riveted her. Nobody told her their plans, which was a painful reminder that she wasn't part of this family or any other.

Tears stung her eyes. She kept them from falling as she turned off the light in the living room before creeping up the stairs. Refusing to look in the mirror over the sink, she got ready for bed. She tiptoed into Olivia's room. The little girl was asleep, her slow, deep breaths loud in the silent room.

Katie Kay crawled into her borrowed bed. The sheets were cool, but the drops running down her cheeks seared her skin. Pressing her face to the pillow, she gave up the battle to hold in her grief.

She was alone. She and the *boppli*.

God is with you always. How many times had she heard that? But why would God offer her comfort when she'd turned away from the life He'd given her?

Once released, her grief and fear refused to be contained. The cotton beneath her cheek grew damp, then wet, and still her tears fell as she mourned for everything that had gone wrong in her life.

A gentle breath brushed her face in the moment before Olivia whispered, "No sad, Kay-Kay." Her tiny hand patted Katie Kay's arm. "No cry, Kay-Kay. Please."

Katie Kay was startled. She hadn't heard the little girl get up. Olivia must have been woken by her sobs. Another mistake to add to her long list.

Rolling over to face the *kind*, Katie Kay whispered, "Aren't you supposed to be asleep?"

"You sad. Wanna hug? A hug makes it better." She held up her short arms.

Suddenly Katie Kay couldn't imagine anything she wanted more than comfort from one small *kind*. Olivia's solace was offered with no strings attached other than her heartstrings, which had been touched by Katie Kay's weeping.

Katie Kay swung her legs over the side of the bed. Picking up the little girl, she set Olivia beside her. Holding out her own arms, she gathered the *kind* close. The aroma of Olivia's flowery shampoo swirled through her senses as she welcomed the hug.

"Danki," she murmured into the *kind*'s silken red hair.

"That means 'thank you,' doesn't it?" Olivia stared at her. "You talk like Uncle Micah."

"I do…sometimes."

"Will you teach me to talk like you?"

"If your *mamm*—your mother—says it's okay." She brushed her tears aside as a smile edged along her lips. Spending time with the inquisitive little girl would help her to stop thinking about her troubles...she hoped.

"*Mamm*. Mommy. *Mamm*. Mom." Olivia giggled and then clamped her pudgy hands over her mouth. Whispering again, she said, "Sounds the same."

"The words do, don't they?" She lifted the *kind* off the bed. "You should get back to bed."

"Mommy sleeps with me when I've gots a bad dream. I stay with you."

Katie Kay bit her lip to keep it from trembling as a new storm of tears filled her eyes. She watched Olivia run to her own bed and collect her pillow. The little girl put it next to Katie Kay's before clambering to sit beside her.

Lying down, Katie Kay blinked hard when the little girl embraced her again. She closed her eyes as she leaned her head on the *kind*'s soft hair. She wasn't sure which of them fell asleep first.

The hope that things would be better after a *gut* night's sleep had been as unreasonable as Katie Kay's expectation that Austin would do the right thing and apologize. Though Olivia's kindness had allowed her to find sleep, reality reared its ugly head again the next morning.

Nothing had changed.

Katie Kay woke with a groan. She heard sounds of the household getting ready for another day. Olivia had returned to her bed sometime during the night, but she was already out of the room. Alone, Katie Kay was tempted to pull the pillow over her head and stay in bed until everyone else left.

Facing Gemma and Sean after last night was impossible. Their acceptance seemed to make the whole situation worse. Everyone was being kind to her. Even Micah, though he'd been blunt about why he'd proposed. But he'd been trying to be nice to her. He hadn't wanted her to have any illusions about why he was proposing.

She couldn't stay in bed. Getting up, she dressed in the clothes Gemma had lent to her. They didn't fit well, and Katie Kay knew—sooner or later—she needed to return to Lancaster and collect her things from Austin's apartment. She wasn't sure when he'd be there. He hadn't worked in the past month. Not like Micah who was successful in his business with Sean Donnelly.

She crossed her arms in front of her as she stared at Olivia's empty bed. She didn't want to think about Micah. It was easier to be angry at him than to wonder what she'd do now that she hadn't accepted his proposal. There had to be someone who'd help.

Because you're cute and a flirt, but you'll soon be fat and nobody will want to flirt with you.

She hated her conscience, but she wouldn't be forced into a loveless marriage. Maybe, before she had told Micah that she didn't want to spend time with him anymore, it might have been possible for her to accept his offer.

Not now.

Not after the cruel and taunting words she'd fired at him.

"Good morning, Katie Kay," called Gemma from the bedroom doorway. She held a bundle of dirty laundry in front of her. "How are you feeling this morning?"

"Fine," she replied, but her stomach roiled as she stood, countermanding her words. Putting her hand over her mouth, she ran to the bathroom.

It was almost ten by the time Katie Kay got downstairs. She glanced toward the kitchen, but the idea of breakfast was nauseating. She'd wait for lunch, and maybe her stomach would have settled by then.

Gemma smiled when Katie Kay came into the living room. "Just in time. You can join us."

"Us?" She glanced around the room, which was empty except for her and her hostess.

"My young mothers' prayer group." Gemma hurried on, warning Katie Kay that her pulse of dismay had been visible on her face. "It's okay. There aren't any plain women among my prayer group friends. I doubt any of them know folks from your district."

"I don't want to intrude."

"You won't." She smiled. "And lurking around in the kitchen will rouse their curiosity. Why don't you join us?"

Katie Kay was tempted to be honest and state she was uncomfortable joining an *Englisch* prayer group. She bit her lip. Until she made up her mind where she intended to live and how, she shouldn't close any doors or alienate anyone, especially the Donnellys, who'd welcomed her as if they'd been friends for years.

She helped Gemma put out plates of cookies and make coffee and tea for the members of the prayer circle. She watched Olivia, hoping the little girl hadn't said anything to her *mamm* about Katie Kay's tears last night. Olivia seemed focused on playing with her little brother, Jayden, as they built buildings out of wooden logs and filled them with plastic horses in the most outrageous pastel shades. They giggled and jumped around as if they were riding the horses.

Gemma paused in her preparations when Olivia dropped her plastic pony and began to cough. Pulling an inhaler out of the pocket of the shirt that was taut across her belly, she inserted it into a tube. She held the tube to Olivia's mouth and told her daughter to breathe deeply. Pressing the inhaler, she calmed the little girl as the medicine hissed into the tube and was drawn into Olivia's mouth and lungs. They repeated the procedure a second time before Gemma led her *kind* into the kitchen and had her wash her mouth out with clean water.

"She has asthma," Gemma said when she caught Katie Kay watching. "When she plays too hard, sometimes she has an attack. Thank the good Lord, her inhaler takes care of it as long as we get to her fast."

"Do you always carry an inhaler?"

She smiled. "Always, and Sean keeps one in the truck." She continued chatting as she finished getting everything ready for her guests.

Katie Kay wanted to tell Gemma she understood what it was like having a special needs *kind* in the house, but such a discussion would have to wait.

The other five women began arriving just before eleven, and each of them seemed to accept Gemma's explanation that Katie Kay was a guest from out of town. The women ranged in age from younger than Katie Kay to their midthirties.

Sitting in the living room, she listened as they spoke about the challenges they faced as mothers. Would she be confronted with the same problems? Not the ones where the women were concerned about their husbands, who were struggling, too, to understand the changes a *boppli* could bring to their lives. When the women bowed their heads to pray, so did Katie Kay, but her heart remained closed. She wasn't sure what would happen if she opened it to God. Would He turn His back on her as Austin had? And as Micah had when she turned down the proposal he'd made out of obligation?

She was surprised that Micah's actions bothered her more than Austin's. It had to be a sign she was too distraught to think clearly.

Katie Kay breathed a sigh of relief when the women turned to the refreshments and conversation. She had the excuse to bring coffee and tea to serve to Gemma's guests. They thanked her and tried to make her feel welcome, but she sensed the questions they didn't utter. She kept up an easy patter to defuse their curiosity.

When everyone was served, she took her chair again and selected a chocolate chip cookie from the plate on the coffee table. Suddenly she was starving. A *gut* sign because her hunger should mean the day's nausea was over.

Gemma's youngest, Jayden, toddled to his *mamm* and climbed onto her lap. Gemma continued her story without a pause but drew the little boy close to her. When he seemed to reshape himself so he could lean against her distended stomach, Katie Kay was startled by her surprising sense of longing.

Would the *boppli* inside her ever reach out to her with such innocent love as Jayden did?

"Mommy gots baby." Jayden patted her stomach and grinned while everyone chuckled.

Sliding off her lap, he went to the brunette whom Katie Kay thought was named Roberta. He tapped her belly as he had Gemma's.

"Gots baby?" he asked.

That brought more laughter, because Roberta looked ready to go into labor at any second.

He started to move to the next woman, who held her

hands in the air and laughed, "No, Jayden. I don't 'gots baby.' Not yet anyhow."

"No baby?" His pudgy face dropped as he turned to Katie Kay.

As she tensed, Gemma scooped him up and cradled him as if he were a *boppli*. "That's enough, young man."

Katie Kay hoped nobody heard her soft sigh of relief that Gemma had halted him before he asked if she had a baby. Too many people already knew. She trusted the Donnellys and Micah to keep her secret, but the more people who discovered she was pregnant, the greater the likelihood that they'd slip and word of her condition would reach her family.

They couldn't know until she told them.

Whenever that might be.

Micah doubted he'd ever understood how deep guilt could go until, that evening after he drove home, he saw a buggy and a familiar horse near the barn on the Stoltzfus family farm. The handsome bay belonged to their bishop, Reuben Lapp.

Katie Kay's *daed*.

For a moment, he was tempted to turn his buggy around and drive in the opposite direction. He pushed that thought aside, knowing that, like Katie Kay, he couldn't avoid her *daed* forever. He drew Rascal to a stop. As he stepped out, he saw his future stepfather emerging from the *dawdi haus*.

Reuben looked every bit the Amish bishop he was. His gray beard hung to the middle of his chest, and his eyebrows were so bushy they seemed to arrive ahead of him. His dark suspenders matched his broadfall trousers and scuffed work boots. In addition to his duties as their bishop, he oversaw his farm, more and more with the help of his son and son-in-law. When he called out a greeting, his deep voice resonated off the nearby barn.

"How goes the solar panel business?" Reuben asked as he waited for Micah to reach him on the lawn beneath a tall maple reaching the apex of its scarlet glory.

"Well." He hated having to force a smile, but he had to. A genuine one wouldn't come because he had to fight to keep from being honest about knowing where Katie Kay was. "Almost too well. A lot of folks, both plain and *Englisch*, want to get panels on their roofs to help offset heating costs this winter."

"The almanac says we could have a snowy winter this year. Will that be a problem?"

"No. Snow melts fast off the panels because they continue to gather the sun's heat through a few inches of snow. With a heavier storm, most homeowners won't have to do more than clear off a corner of a panel. That'll start the snow melting."

Reuben smiled. "They seem to be a true blessing for any of us who don't want to be connected to the grid." He raked his long beard. "Any chance I could pull strings as a soon-to-be family member and get on your schedule to have a couple put on my roof?"

Micah gave in to his laugh. It felt *gut* not to have to weigh every word and expression. "I think Sean and I can squeeze you in, if you don't mind us spreading the job out over a few Saturdays."

"Your partner's wife is going to have a *boppli* soon, ain't so?"

"*Ja*, but not for a couple of months, so we should have plenty of time to get the panels on and hooked up for you."

The bishop's brows lowered. "I didn't realize you did the electrical work, too."

"I don't." He understood what Reuben wasn't saying. A plain craftsman seldom worked with wiring, except to take it out of an *Englisch* house where an Amish family planned to live. "I leave that to Sean. It's his specialty. Mine is getting the panels at the best angle to capture the most sunlight. There's no sense going to the expense of having them installed if the household can't get the most electricity out of them."

"No wonder you're such *gut* partners." Reuben's face cleared, and his easy smile returned. "I'm glad you've worked out your jobs as you have."

"Ja," Micah said again and then waited for the bishop to go on. Reuben wouldn't have brought up the topic if he didn't have something he felt he needed to say about Micah's work with an *Englischer*.

Reuben was blunt. "There have been worries about our young people who are working off their family farms. Any skill a man or woman can learn that is useful in a plain life is welcome, of course. However, some of our young ones are learning things that won't be of any use to them once they're baptized. *Danki* for not sneaking around as others are, Micah."

He nodded but avoided Reuben's steady gaze. If his future stepfather had any idea what Micah was hiding, he wouldn't have given Micah a friendly clap on the shoulder and a cheery farewell before continuing toward his buggy. Reuben waved as he drove away.

Micah watched him go. How much longer was Katie Kay going to quibble over whether she should let her *daed* know where she was? Keeping the secret was eating him from the inside out.

God, You could have put anyone in her way that night. Anyone would have helped her. Why did You choose me? What am I supposed to do? She refused my proposal. What else can I do?

He ignored his conscience, which reminded him how coldly he'd spoken to Katie Kay when he asked her to marry him. But he'd wanted to make sure she knew right from the get-go that he wasn't asking because he loved her. She'd wound him around her little finger once, and he wouldn't be foolish again.

"Are you going to stand there all evening, son?" called *Mamm* from the *dawdi haus* porch.

Pasting another smile on his face and hoping it looked more natural than it felt, he turned to answer her question. He hoped it would be the only one she asked tonight. "Not if you have cookies or pie waiting."

She laughed. "And ruin the supper Leah has cooked for us?"

"A cookie or two has never hurt my appetite."

Again *Mamm* chuckled, and he did, too, though it wasn't easy to make it sound genuine. What would *Mamm* think if she learned of how he had abetted Katie Kay in her secrecy?

Something had to change.

Right away.

Chapter Five

The next morning, at the Donnellys' house, Micah accepted Gemma's invitation to come inside and have a cup of *kaffi* while Sean finished his breakfast. Glancing around the kitchen, he saw no sign of Katie Kay.

"She's been sick every morning," Gemma said when she noticed him looking around. "As I've told her, morning sickness should pass in a week or two."

"I hope she realizes how blessed she is to have you," he said as Jayden crawled in his lap.

The two-year-old wanted to show off the plastic cow he'd found at the bottom of the toy box. Because the little boy hadn't seen it in a few weeks, he was as excited as if it were a brand-new toy.

Across the table, DJ was eating his cereal as if afraid someone was going to snatch it away from him. Drops of milk clung to the table, his chin and the napkin stuck in the neck of his shirt. Olivia nibbled delicately on her toast, and Micah smiled. There was something extra precious about a little girl amidst her rowdy brothers.

A no-longer-unexpected throb of jealousy cut through Micah. He'd hoped to have a family like this— or at least be beginning one—by now. If Katie Kay had been the woman he'd once believed her to be, maybe they would have been working together to have the life Sean and Gemma had.

He pretended to be enthralled with Jayden's black-and-white plastic cow. He realized he was overdoing it when Sean shot him a curious glance. His partner knew him too well, but Sean didn't know the whole truth about how Katie Kay had humiliated him.

As if his thoughts had summoned her, Katie Kay walked into the kitchen. She faltered and gasped when she looked at him.

"I thought you'd left already. That is, I heard—" She fled out of the room.

Setting Jayden on his feet, Micah stood and followed her. He stopped in front of her. If she pushed past him or edged around him, he wouldn't halt her, but he hoped surprise would pause her in her tracks.

It did, and she gave him the frown he was familiar with. The frown told him she didn't want him in her life any longer. Well, too bad. As long as she was living under his friends' roof, she was going to have to put up with seeing him. He'd rescued her from beside the road, so he was responsible for her...as he would have been if she'd been an abandoned kitten. And he couldn't ignore her unborn *boppli*.

"Are you going to keep running away forever?" he asked.

She blanched, and he regretted the words. As he started to apologize, she waved his words aside. "I don't want you lying to me, Micah."

"I don't want to lie either, but I could have been nicer."

"You could have." A faint smile played at the corners

of her mouth. "I'm assuming you have something to say to me other than less-than-nice questions."

"*Ja.* When are you going to see a *doktor*?" He shook his head. "Knowing you, I guess that's not the question I should be asking."

Her whisper of a smile weakened. "No, it's not."

Before she could tell him—again—that he needed to stay out of her life, he hurried to say, "The question I should be asking is, have you seen a *doktor* yet?"

"I just found out I'm… I'm going to have a *boppli*." Color rose in her cheeks with the vibrant pink hue that had fascinated him from the time they were *kinder*. She'd been brimming with excitement back then, and he'd been drawn to the shade like a rabbit into a snare.

Telling himself to focus on the present and forget the past, he said, "You should see a *doktor* or a midwife right away. There's a birthing clinic in Paradise Springs. I'll take you there."

Her face seemed to thin as it paled once more, as if life had been sucked out of her. "I can't go to a clinic in Paradise Springs. Not yet."

He jammed his hands into the pockets of his work coat so she wouldn't see how they curled into frustrated fists. "Stop thinking only of yourself! You need to make sure your *boppli* is growing well."

"I'm not thinking only of myself."

"No?" He was pushing her, but she had to be sensible. Hiding at his friends' house was preposterous. He'd guessed she'd stay with the Donnellys for a night or two and then go home to her own family.

She walked to the front window. When Gemma hurried past them with DJ, making sure he wasn't too late to catch the school bus, Katie Kay didn't turn to look at them or him.

The moment the door closed behind Gemma and her son, Katie Kay said, "All I've been thinking about is the *boppli*. I'm trying to figure out what's best for him or her."

"Keeping the *boppli* away from its family is…" He amended what he was about to say, knowing she wouldn't take it well. "It can't be right."

"I know. It should be simple, but it's not, Micah." She looked at him.

He wondered if he'd ever seen such honest emotion on her face. It revealed the uncertainty she was wrestling with. He was crossing the room to her before he realized what he was doing. He pulled her into his arms and wasn't surprised when his shirt dampened with her tears.

Lord, he prayed, *it hurts to see her brought low. I know she is too proud, but please lift her up so she can see the right way to go.*

A throat was cleared behind him, and he glanced toward the kitchen door to see Sean and the younger kids there. His friend looked concerned, but Micah couldn't guess if his anxiety was for Katie Kay's tears or because Micah was trying to comfort her. Should he have avoided trying to ease her pain?

With a sigh, he knew Katie Kay wasn't the only one who needed to make tough decisions…and stick with them.

Katie Kay wasn't sure how Micah had arranged it, but the following morning, he told her he'd set up an appointment for her in two days at the birthing clinic in Paradise Springs after it closed for the evening.

"That way, nobody will see you go in or out," he said

as he held out the page where he'd written the name of the midwife she would meet with.

Beth Ann Overholt, she read.

"Do you know her?" Katie Kay asked. "Will she say anything to anyone?"

"Beth Ann is a professional and doesn't gossip about her patients. She's delivered several of the *bopplin* for our family." He shook his head. "How did you get suspicious of everyone and everything?"

She looked again, ashamed of what she had to admit. "The hard way. People I trusted turned away from me."

"People? What people other than your ex-boyfriend?"

Astonished, she raised her eyes, and the intensity of his gaze seared her. "Isn't that enough?"

"I don't know."

"Then why are you asking?"

"Because if you keep acting as if you expect to be ambushed any minute, you're never going to fit into our community." He raised one hand to halt her before she could retort. "Don't say it. I know you haven't decided to return to the plain life."

"I haven't."

"But what are your plans if you don't go home?"

Katie Kay was glad when Sean called out from the kitchen to let Micah know he was ready for work. Sean had been avoiding her since he'd witnessed Micah trying to console her yesterday. Her host hadn't said anything, but she caught his glances, swiftly disguised, in her direction. He wanted to make sure she didn't hurt his friend again.

How much did Sean know about what had happened between her and Micah? Enough so he felt protective of his partner.

She should find another place to live, but where? Micah's question echoed in her mind. What *were* her plans if she chose not to return to her *daed*'s house?

Katie Kay knew she couldn't put off making the decision much longer. To do so, she needed to come to terms with her past. Not just with Micah, but with Austin. Being around Micah made her feel confused because he was her sole connection with the life she'd lived until a few months ago.

But it was time to move forward. She owed the *boppli* that much. Hoping she wouldn't regret it, she picked up the telephone and called Austin's number.

"Eyes on the job, Micah," Sean warned.

Micah knew his friend was half joking. All day, he'd been distracted, replaying the conversation he'd had with Katie Kay over and over. The memory of their sharp words matched the tempo of the drill he was using to prepare the roof for the solar panel frames.

When he'd given her Beth Ann's card, she'd seemed... What was the word he was looking for? Not quite relieved, but that was the closest description he could come up with.

If only Sean had waited a couple more minutes before they left for work. Micah had hoped he'd get an answer from Katie Kay about her future plans. He knew he was getting too mixed up in her drama, but how could he walk away when her *daed* was going to marry his *mamm*? And there was the *boppli* to consider. He knew she was in shock about being pregnant, but he couldn't let her risk the little one while she came to terms with her changed life.

"Sorry," Micah said, realizing he'd wandered off into his dilemmas again. "Lost in my thoughts, I guess."

"No need to ask you whom you're thinking about."

Sean adjusted the belt they used to keep them safe on the roof. "Be careful, Micah."

"I'm trying to be."

"Are you? You're getting more involved every day."

"I know." Micah drove the screw into the framework and checked to see if it was square. He hoped Sean didn't push further. In fact, if they weren't standing on a roof, Micah would have found an excuse to walk away and put an end to the conversation.

Sean meant well. Other than his brothers, Sean was the man he trusted most in the world. Yet, Katie Kay was one subject he wasn't ready to talk about with anyone, not even his best friend.

However, Sean didn't seem to feel the same. Shifting the metal framework an inch lower, he asked, "Do you think she'll leave again?"

"I have no idea what she'll do. I learned that last year." He hated the bitterness in his voice, but he'd always been honest with his partner. He wouldn't let Katie Kay's reappearance change that.

"When she dumped you?"

He paused as he was about to screw in the next bolt. Looking at Sean, he asked, "How do you know she dumped me?"

Sean gave a derisive snort. "Man, you've got the truth written all over your face. Every time you see Katie Kay, you either have a lovesick puppy expression or look like you wished you were a million miles from her." He set the bolt he held into the metal beams to connect them together. "Even if I didn't know you'd dated her, I'd know there had been some serious history between you two."

"History is in the past." He said that as much to convince himself as Sean.

And he failed, because his partner said, "But she's here. It's got to mean something."

"Ja." He couldn't argue with that, but he wondered if she would have ever returned if her former boyfriend hadn't forced her out of his car and into her old life.

Micah struggled to keep his mind on the day's tasks. Every hour seemed to drag until it felt like a year. He was clumsy, and more than once, he had to dig another nut or bolt out of his pocket because his numb fingers had dropped the one he held. It wasn't only his fingers that were numb but every inch of him.

The break for lunch didn't help because, as he took a bite of the sandwich with the roast beef his *mamm* had made last night for supper, guilt flashed through him. He'd kept his promise to Katie Kay and hadn't told anyone about her return, but each time he thought about Reuben, he recalled how sad the older man looked whenever someone mentioned his runaway daughter.

"Why don't you come to supper tonight?" Sean asked as they threw their lunch trash into the dumpster in front of the house and put their lunch boxes in the van.

"You don't have to feed me every night."

"I know we don't, but Gemma likes to have a chance to see you, and you know the kids adore you."

"Tell Gemma some other night. *Mamm* mentioned she wanted to discuss her wedding plans with us tonight."

Sean screwed up his face. "Be grateful she doesn't want you to wear a rented monkey suit for the big event."

Micah chuckled because he knew Sean was trying to jest him out of his dismal mood. He played along the rest of the afternoon, but he doubted Sean believed his joking and easy talk about sports and future jobs they had waiting for them.

Why should Sean believe that when Micah didn't?

Chapter Six

Gemma burst out of the house as the Plain and Simple Solutions van pulled into the driveway just past noon the following day. Sean had forgotten his lunch, and Micah wanted to check on Katie Kay. He hadn't seen her that morning before they left for the job site.

Sean muttered something under his breath, and Micah understood when he saw dismay blossoming on his friend's wife's face. Sean didn't like Gemma getting upset now that she was so far along in her pregnancy. Or was his partner distressed because Gemma was running? Micah knew she should be more cautious not to bring on premature labor.

Then he noticed the other side of the driveway was empty. Had Gemma decided to put the family van in the garage with thunderstorms in the forecast?

Throwing open the door, Sean jumped out. "Gemma, is everything okay? Are the kids okay?"

"We're fine." She put her hand on his arm, glancing at Micah as he came around the work van. "My van is gone!"

Micah wondered if his face was as gray as Sean's became.

"Gone?" Sean asked. "Stolen?"

Gemma waved aside his words as ridiculous and then put her hand against the side of her rounded belly. She grimaced.

Sean lifted her as if she weighed no more than one of the pebbles beside the driveway.

Micah hurried to the front door and held it open. When the kids—including DJ, who must have just gotten home from school—crowded into the hall, he shooed them aside. Sean needed to carry Gemma in without tripping over one of the *kinder.*

Once Sean and Gemma had passed him, he shut the door and then rushed to make sure no toys were in Sean's way. Sending DJ for an afghan and Olivia for a pillow, he scooped up Jayden to keep the little boy from being underfoot. He set the toddler on the nearby recliner and motioned for him to stay there. The older *kinder* quickly returned with the items he'd requested. Putting the pillow against one arm of the couch, he stepped back so Sean could set Gemma down. She was protesting that she was fine and she could walk on her own two feet, thank you, but Sean ignored her. He placed her on the cushions as if she were made of precious china. Micah handed him the afghan, and Sean draped it over her legs.

"Mommy!" cried Jayden as he jumped from the chair and ran to her.

Micah halted the *kind* by swinging him into his arms. The little boy giggled, distracted.

"Do I need to call the doctor?" Sean asked.

"No." Gemma rolled her eyes. "Stop overreacting to everything I do or say, Sean. It's not like you're a first-time father. I got a stitch in my side. I haven't run much lately."

"Are you sure?"

"Positive." She squeezed her husband's hand before she looked at Micah. "It's okay. Jayden, come and sit with me." Smiling at her other *kinder*, she motioned for them to join her.

As the youngsters climbed up beside her, Sean said, "As long as you're okay…"

"I am."

"Let's start over. Where's the van, Gemma?"

"I'm not sure." Her gaze shifted to Micah again. "I think Katie Kay has it."

Micah sank to the recliner's arm. "Why do you think that?"

"For one thing, she's not around, and I did tell her the first day she was here that she should feel free to borrow it. I wasn't sure when she planned to see a doctor or if she would want to get some things for herself. She has nothing but the clothes she was wearing and an empty purse. I told her she could use the ready cash in the smallest canister if she needed to buy something." She sighed. "She thanked me and showed me a driver's license, so I figured she knew how to drive. But I also figured she'd let me know before she took the van."

"When did she leave?"

"It must have been while I was taking a morning nap along with the kids. I didn't know the van was gone until DJ got home."

Before he could halt himself, Micah said, "I guess she didn't want to disturb you." He regretted the words as soon as he spoke them because he saw the weight of worry in Gemma's expression. She was less worried about her van than about why Katie Kay had taken it. "I guess she could have left you a note."

"Yes, she could have." Gemma rubbed her forehead. "I'm sorry. I didn't mean to snap at *you*, Micah."

"You've got every right to be annoyed with me. I'm the one who brought her here. I'm sorry to get you caught up in her turbulent life."

"She's mixed-up and scared and feeling alone."

He nodded, agreeing. He'd never imagined Katie Kay Lapp feeling alone. All her life, she'd delighted in being the center of attention, and that had ended. At least for now.

Sean asked, "Could she have gone home?"

"I doubt it," Micah answered. "She's been insistent that she needs time to decide what to say to Reuben, though I don't know why it's taking her so long to realize she doesn't need to say anything other than 'I'm sorry' and 'Forgive me.'" Looking at Gemma, he asked, "Have you reported the van missing?"

"Of course not! If Katie Kay has it, and I'm sure she does, I don't want her being pulled over by the cops. I know you Amish don't like having police involved in your problems, Micah."

He understood what Gemma was trying to avoid saying. She was most worried about upsetting him. Wanting to thank her and reassure her that nothing Katie Kay did was a surprise any longer, he went into the kitchen to get Sean's lunch box. The Donnellys needed time to talk without him there.

As he picked up the battered box, he wondered how Katie Kay could have taken Gemma's van without asking. He hadn't thought Katie Kay was that selfish. What was so pressing she couldn't wait long enough to let someone know she was borrowing it?

The search for answers taunted Micah the rest of the day. He tried to concentrate on work, because he could see Sean was having a tough time doing the same. When the distant rumble of thunder signaled they had to get off the roof, they collected their tools and scurried down the ladders. Micah sent up a silent prayer of gratitude.

They gathered the ladders to put them onto the rack on top of the van. As they were loading the last ladder, Sean's cell phone rang with the melody that meant Gemma was calling. Micah froze and then shoved the ladder into place. He lashed the bungee cords around it while his partner answered the call.

"It's Gemma," Sean said unnecessarily and then continued to listen to his wife. "She's back."

Hoping he wasn't misunderstanding, Micah asked, "Katie Kay?"

He got a nod in response.

Sean ended the call and motioned for Micah to get in the van. A few raindrops struck the windshield, but the storm went north as they sped south toward the Donnellys' house. Sean said nothing, and Micah did the same though curiosity taunted him.

Where had Katie Kay gone? Why? Was she back to stay? Was she ready to go home and face the rest of her life? Or was she there only to return Gemma's van and planned to leave for *gut*?

He was shocked at how the thought of losing her again was more painful than he'd expected. His efforts to banish her from his heart hadn't been as thorough as he'd bragged to himself. After accusing her of having too much *hochmut*, pride had misled *him*.

Sean was out of the van the moment he thrust the shift into park. He started for the house and then paused.

"What's wrong?" Micah asked.

"Someone hit the van." He bent to run his fingers

along a dent in the bumper. Straightening, he raced to the house.

Micah wanted to follow him and get answers, but he knew the couple needed a minute or two to talk before he burst in. He knelt by the van and examined the damage. Running his fingers along the dent as Sean had, he smiled grimly. It was minor. The dent could be knocked out easily. It wouldn't need much more than a little chrome paint to touch it up, and nobody would ever notice the difference.

He hoped he could say the same for the harm Katie Kay might have done to herself in the Donnellys' eyes.

And his.

Was she always going to be thoughtless and selfish?

He pondered that as he entered the house just in time to hear Gemma sigh.

"I don't know what happened," she said as he joined her and Sean in the kitchen. "She didn't say a single word to me or the kids. She didn't look hurt. Not physically anyhow. When I went out to talk to her, I saw the damage to the van. By the time I'd finished examining the dent, she was gone."

"Gone?" Micah asked. "She ran away again?"

Gemma aimed a frown at him. "Why must you think the worst of her, Micah?"

"Me?" He was shocked she'd turned her frustration on him. "She busted your van."

"It's a teeny dent. Nothing more. I thought you'd be more forgiving."

"Because I'm Amish?"

Her scowl deepened. "No, because you once were in love with her. She went to the swimming hole. I think she wanted to be alone to think."

A glance out the window over the sink revealed that

Katie Kay still stood by the pond Sean had dug out a few summers ago to make a swimming hole for his kids. He'd stocked it with small fish the *kinder* could catch and release.

"As long as nobody was hurt," Sean said as he held out his arms.

As Gemma threw herself into Sean's embrace, Micah knew he should be somewhere else. Making sure he had his irritation with Katie Kay under control, he left the kitchen and crossed the yard toward her. The thunder was fading over the hills, and the air hung with a clammy dampness that suggested more storms were heading their way. He doubted they could be stronger than the one inside him.

He thought she was tossing pebbles into the water, but, as he got closer, he saw she was shredding a bright orange leaf. She must have heard him approach through the crackle of the fallen leaves, but she didn't look at him.

Stopping beside her, he remained silent. He bent and picked up a flat stone. He sent it skipping across the pond that reflected the gray sky. When she didn't react, he chose a second and then a third and watched them skim the water. The pond rippled, though he knew it was quiet beneath.

The opposite of Katie Kay who appeared calm, save for a faint quiver in her fingers as she ripped the leaf to smaller and smaller pieces. She hunched into herself.

"You owe Gemma an explanation," he said when he couldn't endure the silence any longer.

She looked at him. "Don't, Micah. I don't need you yelling at me."

"I'm not yelling. I haven't raised my voice."

"Maybe not, but you're angry."

His brows lowered as he wondered how she expected him to feel when she'd acted outrageously. "Of course I'm angry. Gemma agreed to let you use her van. Not only did you take it without letting her know, you dented it."

"I would have told her, but she was taking a nap, and I didn't want to disturb her. I didn't realize I'd be gone so long." She clasped her hands in front of her as she added, "And for your information, I didn't dent the van. Someone ran into it while it was parked."

He believed her. Katie Kay had never lied to get herself out of trouble. "Where did you go?"

"Where else? Lancaster."

Astonishment ripped through him. She'd gone to the city? Back to the man whose name she seldom mentioned? Was she, as he'd thought earlier, at the Donnellys' only to say good-bye?

Katie Kay watched as Micah closed his mouth that had become a circle of surprise. He was trying to keep his promise that he wouldn't yell at her, but anger blazed from his eyes.

"Go ahead," she said when he didn't speak.

"With what?"

"Your questions about why I went to Lancaster."

"I don't need to ask. I think it's pretty obvious. You went to see the *daed* of your *boppli*, didn't you?"

"I did." She didn't let her eyes shift away from his intense gaze.

He took a single step toward her, but she wouldn't let him intimidate her. The thought startled her. When had Micah become her enemy? Their friendship had been destroyed when she stopped walking out with him, but he'd never been her foe.

Not as Austin had become.

No! She wasn't going to let either man unsettle her more. Nothing had gone as she'd hoped, but she'd done her best. Yet, just as when she'd tried to take care of *Daed*'s house, her best hadn't been *gut* enough.

"You've changed, Micah. You used to give me the benefit of the doubt. Now you assume I'm irresponsible."

"It's not that."

"No?"

A flush rose out of the collar of his work coat. She'd made her point, but she didn't feel any triumph.

His mouth grew taut again. "No, Katie Kay, it's not that."

"Then what?"

"How would you feel if someone you were responsible for went missing and you had no idea where he or she was?"

"You're not responsible for me."

"I'm not talking about me." He gestured toward her middle. "What if your little *boppli* vanished and you didn't know where to begin to look?"

Each word struck like the thunder resounding over the hills. She clasped her fingers protectively over her abdomen. The thought of losing the *boppli* made her stomach twist. Realizing what she was doing, she let her hands drop to her sides. She mustn't give Micah—or anyone else—a clue to her greatest fear. The fear that, despite him not wanting anything to do with her or their *kind*, Austin might demand she turn their *boppli* over to him. What if he decided having a *kind* of his own made him look cool in his friends' eyes?

"I'm sorry. I should have told Gemma. I'll tell her

I'm sorry, Micah," she said in a cool tone she hoped he'd misunderstand.

When he did, she was torn between relief and regret. Relief that she'd refocused the conversation on the van instead of the *boppli*, but regret that he seemed eager to see the worst side of her.

"I'm not sure Gemma will ever trust you again," he said.

"I know."

"What was so important you couldn't take time to jot a note to let her know where you were going?" His eyes narrowed. "Why were you eager to see the man who dumped you on the side of the road?"

She flinched. Micah said what he thought, but his comments used to be softened by her knowing he never meant to cause hurt. Today, she wasn't so sure.

"I found out Austin was at home. I know I was a fool to rush to Lancaster to try to get my things. When I got there, he agreed to talk to me, but he didn't let me into the apartment." She lowered her eyes, not willing to see the pity in Micah's.

She wasn't going to tell him how embarrassed she'd felt to stand in the dirty hallway and beg for her possessions. Nor would she reveal how Austin had refused to give them to her. Vinnie, one of his friends, had sneaked down the fire escape with a small bag of her clothes. Not everything, and she guessed the rest had been claimed by others. Nobody had wanted the plain dress she'd brought with her from Paradise Springs, so it was at the bottom of the plastic bag.

"You hoped he'd ask your forgiveness for his outrageous behavior, ain't so?"

"I don't know. If I did, I was disappointed. He didn't apologize, and then everything got worse." She wrapped her arms around herself. "No, it went from worse to worst."

"Why?"

For a second, she hesitated; then the words spilled out of her. "He told me if I wanted to get rid of 'the kid'—that's what he calls the *boppli*—he'd be willing to give me money to hire a lawyer to arrange for an adoption." She couldn't keep her rancor out of her voice as she added, "He said it was my fault so I should pay for most of it. Before he slammed the door in my face, he said if the *boppli*'s new parents gave me any money, he wanted half."

"Is giving the *boppli* up for adoption what you plan to do? Or have you given that any real thought?"

For the first time, she met his eyes steadily. "Do you think so little of me, Micah Stoltzfus? This *boppli* is my responsibility, and I'm going to make sure it has the best life possible." She released a terse laugh. "Besides, I know Austin was lying. He'll never send me a penny for anything. I left and went back to the van. That's when I found the dent in the front and the policeman."

"It was hit while you were parked?"

She nodded. "The officer said the kid who hit it was going too fast in the wrong direction along the one-way street. When he saw another car pull in to the street, he panicked and tried to turn around. He hit the van. The officer said if Gemma had a more modern car, the whole front end would have been smashed like the kid's car. Instead there's a small dent."

"Was the other driver hurt?"

"Not according to the policeman. I guess the *gut* Lord was watching over us." She was astonished by the warmth surging through her at the thought. Was it possible God still cared about His lamb who had strayed so far from the flock?

As if she'd asked that aloud, Micah said, "None of us should ever doubt that, Katie Kay. No matter what we do or where we go, God is just a prayer away. You're never alone."

"It didn't feel that way when I was talking to Austin." She flung the remainder of the leaf into the pond. "I should have known he wouldn't change his mind. He's as stubborn as..."

"You?"

She glanced at his face, hoping to see the charming smile he had worn when he walked out with her. Instead he remained as serious as a deacon facing a miscreant who'd ignored the *Ordnung*.

"Ja," she said with a sigh. The conversation wasn't going as she'd hoped. She hadn't expected Micah to take her in his arms and console her as he had before, but why did he have to be stonyhearted? "One thing I know for sure is that I can close the door on that part of my past."

"Are you sure? He is your *boppli*'s *daed*."

"Didn't you hear what I said?" she asked, feigning irritation to conceal her deep fear that Austin would decide to claim the *kind* and take it away from her. "He wanted me to get rid of it. He doesn't care about the *boppli* or me."

He arched his brows. "People change their minds."

"If you're trying to scare me, Micah, don't bother. I'm scared enough already."

For a long minute, he didn't answer. He sighed and said, "Let's go. It looks as if it's going to storm any minute." He turned to leave.

She didn't move. "Micah?"

"Ja?" He halted but didn't face her.

Just as she hadn't turned to him when he came to the pond. The barriers between them were growing thicker and more impossible to cross. Maybe he realized that, too, which was why he kept his back to her.

"Please," she said as she walked to where he stood, "don't tell Gemma and Sean what I was doing in Lancaster."

"The van—"

"I'll explain to them how the van was dented. I've got a copy of the accident report so they can contact their insurance company. That's what the policeman told me to do. I don't want them to know…"

"How your *boppli*'s *daed* shut you out of his life?"

"Ja." It was humiliating. "Promise me, Micah, you won't tell them."

"I won't." Finally he looked at her. "I'll leave that for you to do."

As he strode away, she remained where she was and watched him go. He always seemed to know exactly what to do. Meanwhile, she was foundering. She'd considered Micah's well-mapped-out life to be boring. For the first time, she guessed there must be a lot of comfort in being prepared for what lay ahead.

Was it too late for her to find out? She hoped not.

Chapter Seven

The birthing clinic was in a low, white building that looked as if it had been built as an *Englisch* ranch house. Shutters the color of pine needles flanked the windows, but the flower boxes were empty. A wreath of autumn leaves and miniature plastic pumpkins was centered on the yellow door. To its left, a small plaque was etched with Paradise Springs Birthing Center.

Katie Kay sat in Micah's buggy and stared at the clinic's front door. She didn't want to look at him. Was he thinking as she was of the night he'd told her about the future he envisioned with her? A future when they were married and had a family. Had he imagined himself bringing her to the midwife when she became pregnant?

How earnest and eager he'd been as he outlined every day of the life he wanted them to have together! So earnest and eager he hadn't noticed her reaction. She'd been horrified. How could she be certain she wanted to spend her life with Micah Stoltzfus when there was much she hadn't experienced? What if she missed wonders she couldn't even imagine?

She'd interrupted him and asked him to take her

home. Though he'd been startled, he'd complied. He'd loved her then. She'd known that, which had unsettled her more.

Once she got home, she'd told him they were through. He'd asked why, and she'd just said she'd decided she didn't want to walk out with him any longer. It hadn't been the truth. She hadn't wanted to break up, but the only thing she'd been sure of was that she needed to sample what else life might offer her.

For days afterward, she'd tried to forget the pain on his expressive face when he turned without another word and climbed into his buggy and drove away. She'd wondered if she'd made the biggest mistake of her life but convinced herself the worst error she could make was always to question if a plain life had been right for her. Once she was baptized and married, there would be no escape without being shunned and losing contact with her family and the community.

But isn't that what you've done to yourself? She wished the faint voice of honesty would leave her alone, but it was true she'd self-shunned by not letting her family know where she moved to in Lancaster.

Again the idea of her mapping out her future flitted through her head. Could she? Should she? If she set a plan in stone as Micah seemed to, what if something marvelous popped up in her life? She didn't like the idea of having to pass it by because it wasn't part of "The Plan."

"The longer you sit there," Micah said, breaking into her thoughts, "the more likely it is that someone will drive by and recognize you."

His words jolted her, and she climbed out of the buggy, almost tripping over her own feet. As she regained her balance, she was startled to discover gentle fingers on her arm. How had Micah gotten around the buggy so fast?

"Danki," she whispered as she stepped away from his touch, which scrambled her thoughts like a bowl of eggs.

Her hopes that he hadn't noticed the tremor in her voice faded when he said, "It's going to be okay." He flashed her a smile.

She was astonished by the warmth stirring in her stomach. Lost in her despair, she'd failed to see how much power his easy grins still had to move her. They weren't flirtatious, but seeing one made her think about how they'd laughed together after singings. Laughing was something they'd done a lot, and she realized how much she missed that simple delight.

Something else she'd thrown away when she tossed him out of her life.

"Tell me the truth, Micah," she blurted. "Why are you helping me?"

"Why wouldn't I? You're pregnant and—"

"But you could let others help. You don't have to feel obligated because you happened to be the one who found me."

He shook his head, sadness dimming his eyes. "After all this time, Katie Kay, I thought you knew me better than that."

She winced. His quiet, sorrowful words hurt as much as if he'd yelled them. She realized how much her question had wounded him. It hadn't been intentional. She wanted to know the truth about why a man whom she'd treated poorly would step up to help her.

No, it was more than helping. He wanted to be certain she and the *boppli* were taken care of and remained healthy. He was a *gut* man. A better man, she acknowledged, than she deserved, because she wasn't sure that if their situations were reversed, she would have been as forgiving.

He didn't say anything else as he opened the door and motioned for her to go inside ahead of him.

Katie Kay was relieved to see the waiting room was empty. It was long and narrow with six plastic chairs along each side of the space. A desk at the far end by a closed door was empty, but she guessed the receptionist usually sat there. Everything about the room exuded happiness and excitement. Too bad she didn't feel either. Uncertainty was the one emotion roiling within her.

When Micah closed the door, he drew the curtain over the window. The others were shut, she noticed with relief. Nobody driving by and looking into the clinic would see them.

"We might as well sit," he said. "Beth Ann told me we'd have to wait while she finished the day's paperwork."

She chose a red chair. "There must be paperwork for me to fill out. Do you know where it is?"

"It's been handled."

"What?"

Taking the chair beside hers, he leaned toward her. "When I explained the situation to Beth Ann, she assured me you could take the paperwork with you and fill it out before your next visit. It's not as if you have health insurance as *Englischers* do." His brow threaded in bafflement. "Or do you?"

"No. My jobs in Lancaster were part-time and paid under the table because I didn't have a social security number card."

"I assume you don't have any savings then."

"Nothing." She looked at her clasped hands. "I know

it's not cheap to pay for a midwife. That's why I'm going to talk to Beth Ann about how long it'll be safe for me to wait on tables."

"You're planning to get a job?" He regarded her with narrowed eyes.

"Of course. The costs of these visits and the delivery will be my obligation, and I need to repay Sean and Gemma for the damage to their van."

"I can fix it. It'll take just a few minutes. Don't worry."

"But it's my fault." Waving aside his argument before he could speak it, she added, "Besides, I've worked all my life, Micah. I'm not doing anything other than helping Gemma keep the house clean, cook a few meals and watch over the kids."

"Which the Donnellys appreciate. Gemma has told me the house has never looked better."

But it wouldn't meet her older sister's standards. She sighed as she imagined Priscilla's comments about the mess Katie Kay found herself in. Her exacting sister held everyone up to her ideas of perfection, and Katie Kay had longed to meet them, so her *daed* and the rest of the family didn't have to worry about the house. She'd failed time after time.

Not wanting to admit that to Micah, she said, "Maybe so, but the tasks at the Donnellys don't keep me busy enough."

"No matter how busy you get, you can't escape your thoughts."

She stared, stunned. Was that what she was doing? Working hard so she was exhausted enough to sleep the instant her head touched the pillow? Focusing on tasks to keep her mind from wandering to her troubles? She had thought her yearning for a job was so she could pay for what she and the *boppli* would need during the next nine months.

Now she wasn't sure.

She was relieved when the door across from the empty desk opened, and a woman stepped out. She didn't have to reply to Micah's too-insightful comment.

The woman introduced herself as Beth Ann. Much taller than Katie Kay, she wore a Mennonite *kapp* like the ones Katie Kay had seen at the Central Market in Lancaster when she went to get fresh vegetables for Austin and his roommates on the few occasions when she had money for such luxuries. Beth Ann's dark blue dress reached below her knees but didn't hide the plastic brace she wore on her right leg. She walked with a hint of a limp as she asked Katie Kay to come with her.

"I'll wait here," Micah said.

Words failed Katie Kay when she stood. For a moment, she wanted to ask him to come with her. Talking to a midwife made the *boppli* real, something she couldn't pass off as a bad dream she'd soon wake up from.

"It'll be fine, Katie Kay," he continued in the same gentle voice. "*You* will be fine."

Was the emphasis to reassure her, or was he talking about both her and the *boppli*?

She had to stop trying to find ulterior meanings in every word everyone around her said, especially Micah. Easier said than done.

Following Beth Ann through the doors, she thanked the midwife for staying late.

"I don't mind," Beth Ann replied. "But I can do this only once in a while because I've got a daughter at home who frets if I'm late often."

Katie Kay nodded. She hadn't expected that Beth

Ann would see her after regular office hours every time, but what she said complicated matters. Coming during the day meant being seen by someone who knew her or her *daed*.

You could go home.

The words were as clear in her mind as if Beth Ann had spoken them, but the midwife was silent until they paused by a set of scales with a digital readout. Katie Kay stepped onto them. Beth Ann noted the number and also ascertained her height before motioning to come farther along the silent hallway.

Going into an examination room painted a warm cream, Beth Ann pulled on a white coat and settled a stethoscope around her neck. She smiled as she motioned for Katie Kay to sit.

"On the table?" Katie Kay asked.

"*Ja*, while I check your heartbeat and the *boppli*'s. After that, you can sit on a chair if you'd rather. This appointment is for us to get to know each other, so you're comfortable with me when it's time to give birth. I'll also have to take blood for a few tests."

"Will they show if the *boppli* has any birth defects?"

Beth Ann rested one hand on the table. "Are there many *bopplin* in your family born with defects?"

"One I know about. My youngest sister died when she was almost four years old. She was born with multiple handicaps, and my parents considered it a blessing she survived as long as she did so we could have her in our lives."

"Tell me about the problems she was born with."

Katie Kay began to list the challenges Sarann had endured. Her little sister had never learned to sit by herself and had to be fed through a special tube in her stomach. Someone had to be with her always. Katie Kay had treasured her times with Sarann because the one thing her little sister did well was smile. Nobody knew if Sarann understood anything said to her, but it didn't matter. Seeing her brilliant smile was like beholding the face of their Heavenly Father shining through her.

Their *mamm* had never once uttered a word of complaint about the long hours of caring for a *kind* who couldn't do anything for herself. Instead, *Mamm* had made sure Sarann shared every experience with the rest of the family. *Mamm* took Sarann to church Sunday services, at least for the first hymns because the little girl seemed to be soothed by the *Leit* combining their voices in slow unity to praise the Lord.

Katie Kay had adored her little sister, and she'd feared her heart would never heal after Sarann's death. *Mamm*'s passing a few years later had changed everyone in the family more than any of them wanted to admit. *Daed* had thrown himself into his work on the farm and as bishop. She'd struggled to meet the high standards set by her older sister and tried to oversee her younger sisters, who were having as much trouble with their grief as she was.

Mamm had been strong while dealing with Sarann. Katie Kay wondered if she could be the same. No, she couldn't. *Mamm* had *Daed* and the rest of the family—as well as a powerful faith—to hold her up. Katie Kay was alone, though she hoped God would eventually welcome her among those He loved.

You are among those He loves. Go home to be with them.

Ach, how she was coming to hate her conscience that spoke at the most unexpected times! It made everything sound simple. Go home as she had the other times she'd left to stay with her *Englisch* friend, but it wasn't straightforward this time.

The problems she'd left behind were waiting for her to face them. She couldn't deny that. She hadn't figured out how to deal with Micah. It would have been much easier if his glance didn't cause a once-familiar ripple of emotion to reach to her toes and fingertips.

Odd that she'd never felt anything similar with Austin.

What was she doing? She should focus on what the midwife said.

"Is it possible this *boppli* will be born with the same problems Sarann had?" she asked.

"Anything is possible, Katie Kay. That's why we must put our faith in God. He—and He alone—can see beyond this moment. He knows and loves your *boppli*. He will never—"

"Don't say it!" Katie Kay was sorry for her outburst the moment the words were out of her mouth, but she'd been unnerved by how Beth Ann's words matched her own thoughts.

The midwife looked at her as if she'd turned into a wild beast. "Say what?"

"God will give us nothing more than we can handle."

Beth Ann frowned. "I wasn't going to say that."

"Oh, sorry. I thought—"

"What I was going to say is God won't ever give us more than we can handle with His help."

Katie Kay bit her lip, not wanting to retort that she didn't want to hear that either. Getting off on the wrong foot with the midwife who'd done her such a great favor by seeing her after-hours would be ludicrous.

She submitted to the examination and listened to Beth Ann's instructions for what to expect as her body changed. She agreed to make an appointment to return in two weeks for a more thorough exam but otherwise spoke only when Beth Ann asked her a direct question. The midwife believed God stood beside Katie Kay. How she wished she could believe that, too!

Chapter Eight

In Katie Kay's opinion, every adult at the table that evening deserved an award for their acting. She'd learned about movie award shows from Cherokee, Vinnie's girlfriend, who was fascinated with everything Hollywood. Katie Kay doubted those excellent actors and actresses would have been able to show such feigned enthusiasm for the stilted conversation at the table as the Donnellys, Micah and she did. Everyone acted as if nothing out of the ordinary had happened.

She'd played her part. She'd bowed her head while Sean said grace. That he spoke aloud was something she found disconcerting, because it was a reminder of how different this household was from the one where she grew up. Her *daed* had bowed his head in silent prayer before and after each meal, and the family did the same.

Yet it was nice to share prayers. While she lived in Lancaster, she'd seen the curiosity aimed in her direction when she bowed her head before she ate at the restaurant where she worked. She wasn't the only one who thanked God for a meal, but everyone there knew she'd been raised Amish. They watched what she did to see if it matched what was on reality shows about people who claimed to be plain.

As the evening meal progressed, Katie Kay smiled when one of the *kinder* told a silly story, and she passed the serving bowls whenever anyone asked. She insisted on clearing the table and putting the dishes into the dishwasher, so Gemma could have time with her husband and *kinder*.

When Katie Kay lingered rinsing out the cooking pots, nobody came to ask what was taking so long. Tears welled into her eyes when she heard the laughter from the other room. The Donnellys were a family, loving each other and spending time together each day. Micah had become part of their family, too, the *onkel* who offered a knee for a *kind* to perch on. Once, she'd had that sense of family; then her *mamm* died and she'd gone from being a *kind* to a surrogate *mamm*.

How had her older sister, Priscilla, made the transition when *Daed*'s first wife passed away? Katie Kay had hoped in the days after *Mamm*'s funeral that Priscilla would give her hints of how to manage, but her sister had acted as if the answer should be obvious…if Katie Kay worked harder. She'd tried but never matched her older sister's skills at cleaning a house or canning garden vegetables or making a cake.

Another failure.

She wiped away dampness from the corners of her eyes. Beth Ann and Gemma had warned her tears were a common side effect of pregnancy, especially in the early months. She was glad—for once—to be alone.

Micah listened to his friends talk and laugh, but his ears strained for the sound of Katie Kay's footsteps. She was taking too long to clean up after the meal. He guessed she was trying to avoid them. All of them or just him? On the way home from the birthing clinic, she hadn't said more than a handful of words, and those had been to thank him for making the appointment and driving her there. She hadn't looked in his direction through the whole meal. He worried when she became taciturn.

Then he heard the soft sound of her sneakers. He didn't look over his shoulder, not wanting to spook her.

Instead he listened as Gemma laughed. "As you know, Micah, Sean and I have had a long discussion about what we'll name the baby. A very long one."

"Which she won as always, so the new baby will be called Dylan." Sean patted his wife's hand. "A wise man knows when the route to victory is surrender."

As they continued to tease each other, Micah risked a glance toward where Katie Kay stood in the doorway between the living room and the kitchen. Her face was blank, but she had laced her fingers together and leaned forward as if she wanted to absorb the love swirling around Sean and Gemma. That, he could understand.

How many times had he wondered what it would be like to have someone love him as Gemma did his partner? Only he and his brother Jeremiah remained unattached among the Stoltzfus siblings. He was very happy his brothers and sisters had found love but yearned for the same for himself.

Once upon a time, he'd thought he'd found true love with Katie Kay. No longer. When she'd tossed him aside as if he were last week's newspaper, he'd closed his heart like a shop shuttered and out of business.

Yet, when he saw her in his friends' living room, he couldn't help feeling sorry for her. She was so alone and too stubborn to admit that she didn't need to be if she returned to her own family.

When Katie Kay sat in a chair behind his, Olivia scrambled down from Sean's lap and crawled into Katie Kay's. Gemma and Sean exchanged a look. Were they worried about their daughter getting attached to Katie Kay or glad that Olivia eased her obvious loneliness?

Again he wondered what would have happened if he'd insisted Katie Kay let him take her home that rainy night. She was impetuous, but he found himself thinking he'd given in to her because he wanted to spend more time with her.

As soon as Gemma announced it was time for the *kinder* to go to bed, Olivia gave Katie Kay a hug before going with her parents. The boys followed.

Before Katie Kay could disappear, too, Micah said, "Let's talk outside while they get the kids ready for bed."

"I thought—I mean, it's late, so I assumed—"

"I'm going to be heading home, if that's what you're trying to ask, but I thought we could talk a few minutes." He stood and motioned toward the kitchen. "It's a nice night. Let's talk while I get Rascal hitched to the buggy."

He thought she might refuse, but she said, "What do you want to talk about?"

"You choose."

He could tell that startled her, because her steps faltered as they went into the kitchen. She hurried past him and pulled the windbreaker Gemma had lent her out of the closet by the back door. As she slipped it on, she said, "Okay. We'll talk about you."

"Me?"

"Sure. Tell me about how you got into installing solar panels."

He shrugged and picked up another cookie as he

walked out with her. Gemma's baking wasn't as *gut* as his *mamm*'s, but he never passed up her chocolate chip cookies…or anyone else's.

The night was cool but not cold as the past few had been. The threat of a hard freeze had passed temporarily. Despite that, he glanced at Katie Kay to check her coat was zipped. He buttoned the top button on his own coat as he followed her down the steps.

Light from the waxing moon glittered off the dew scattered across the lawn. The silhouettes of the garage and the two vans concealed his buggy and Rascal, who must be eager to return to his warm stall.

As they walked on the wet grass, he said, "I feel like I'm serving God by helping others use the gift He created on the very first day."

"You're talking about light." The edge had left her voice, and he guessed he'd surprised her with his answer.

"*Ja*. There's something wondrous about light, which has shone since the beginning and hasn't abated once. It's waiting for us to use it as a precious legacy from the earliest moments of Creation." He grinned. "At least you aren't laughing."

"Why would I laugh? God gave Adam and Eve dominion over His creation and urged them—and their descendants—to use what He'd created. A gift that keeps on giving." She smiled and then laughed. "Something I heard *Englischers* say at the Central Market in Lancaster, and I liked it."

"I like it, too. A gift that never runs out. Sunlight is that, so I can't think of a reason not to use it."

"Especially since the bishops have approved solar on plain houses."

"Not all of them, but many are seeing the light."

When she groaned at his pitiful pun, he chuckled. He was relieved they could laugh together again. After she'd been silent on the way back from Paradise Springs, he hadn't been sure if they could salvage their fragile friendship.

He almost laughed again, but this time with regret because their relationships had teetered on the brink of disaster. And he had to admit, as he hadn't wanted to before, that the uncertainty hadn't always been her doing.

When he whistled, Rascal appeared out of the darkness. Sean had set aside a pasture for the horse and the pony he kept promising Olivia. Micah guessed his friend would want his help finding a gentle-spirited one that wouldn't bite the *kinder*.

"Before you go," Katie Kay said as he led Rascal to the buggy, "I'd like to say something."

"Go ahead."

"I appreciate—no, that's not right. I *needed* to hear what you said before we went into the clinic this evening. You've done so much for me. *Danki*."

As he set Rascal into place and secured him to the buggy, he said, "You don't have to thank me for doing what friends do."

She glanced at the house, which was brightly lit upstairs. "I am grateful to the Donnellys, too."

"They're *gut* people."

"*Ja*. They try to make me feel like family."

As he watched, the window of the boys' room went dark. "That's their way."

"But not everyone's." She wrapped her arms around herself as he stepped from the buggy and faced her. "It's special to have the chance to be with a loving family again. I've missed that."

He frowned, though he wasn't sure if she could see

his expression in the moonlight. "If you miss being around a family, why don't you go home to yours?"

"I told you I need time to figure out what I'm going to do."

"You're going to go or you're going to stay, ain't so?"

She stepped away from him. "It's easy for you to say, but it isn't that easy for me to decide, Micah."

"Why not? You need to do what's right for your *boppli*."

"I am! I don't need to explain myself to you, Micah Stoltzfus!"

Before he could say another word, she whirled and ran into the house. He expected her to slam the door in her wake, but she closed it quietly. Because she knew the *kinder* might already be asleep?

He sighed. It wasn't for him to judge her and her intentions. That was God's task.

"You're being really tough on her," said Sean as he emerged from the shadows by the garage.

"You heard?"

"Yeah. I didn't mean to eavesdrop, but…"

Micah waved aside his words. "It wasn't as if we were whispering."

"One thing I've learned is the most even-tempered woman can be volatile when pregnant." He glanced in the direction of the van Katie Kay had borrowed. "Katie Kay hasn't had a great week." He put his hand on Micah's shoulder. "If you want my advice, give her a break. Yourself, too."

"Me?"

"You've apologized to me at least two dozen times about a tiny dent, and I've told you every time it's okay." He gave a half laugh. "You Amish don't have a monopoly on forgiving others."

Micah sighed at the truth in his friend's words. "Or being grateful for forgiveness when it's offered." He stared at the house. "Or wondering why it hasn't been offered."

"Micah, if you want my opinion, you've gotten too wound up in Katie Kay's problems. She's made it clear she doesn't want your help when it comes to reconciling with her family. Why don't you back off until she figures out what she wants to do?"

"You're right, and taking your advice is the least I can do after you've taken her in, Sean. I never intended for her to stay here past that first night."

"Gemma told me how she appreciates having company during the day. Someone who discusses something other than *Sesame Street* and what color was used in kindergarten that day."

"I'm glad." He rubbed the bridge of his nose. "I need to let her get over visiting the midwife, as well as whatever happened in Lancaster." He almost revealed what Katie Kay had told him, but he wouldn't break the promise he'd made to her.

Sean gave him a half smile. "Another thing I've learned through Gemma's pregnancies is to avoid arguing with her when her hormones are raging. You're smart to let Katie Kay come to terms with being pregnant."

Micah flinched as he did each time someone spoke of the baby who belonged to Katie Kay and her unfeeling *Englischer*. "I see your point."

He did, though he wished Katie Kay would ease Reuben's worries about her. Yet, he knew she needed to make the decision for herself.

Why don't you help her see what's right instead of pushing her to do what you *think she should do?*

That thought surprised him. Why wasn't he helping her discover what God's will was for her? Wasn't assisting one another what the *gut* Lord taught His *kinder* to do?

"Good," Sean said, interrupting Micah's musings. He turned toward the house, and Micah heard a tapping at a kitchen window. "Looks like Gemma's ready to call it a day, too." He started to leave and then paused. "By the way, I forgot earlier. She wants to know if you're planning to join us a week from Saturday at the harvest festival in Exton."

"Wouldn't miss it."

"Glad to hear it." Sean clapped him on the shoulder. "Safe drive home. See you in the morning. We should be able to finish the house by the end of tomorrow. It'll be good to move on to the next, and Gemma told me a couple more people have called and want to talk to us about installing solar panels. Will you have time tomorrow if she can set up appointments for us?"

"*Ja*. I'll let *Mamm* know I'll be late for supper tomorrow night."

"Plan on eating with us." He raised his hands. "Don't say it. Gemma likes having you here to keep the kids occupied."

"In that case, I accept. *Gut nacht*."

Sean hurried into the house, and Micah climbed into his buggy. As he drove along the moonlit roads toward his family's farm, he realized he hadn't asked Sean if Katie Kay was also joining the family at the harvest festival. He hoped so. Only to the moon and to God would he admit he looked forward to spending more time with her to learn about what she wanted and needed in the future for her and her *boppli*.

He knew what he wanted. He wanted to hear her

laugh again as she had when they walked out together. Would her eyes sparkle as they used to when he teased her? He couldn't wait to find out.

Chapter Nine

Why did they run out of parts at the worst possible moment?

Groping in his tool belt pocket for another bolt, Micah appraised the metal structure that would support the solar panels on Reuben's roof. He and Sean had started working at the bishop's house early that Saturday morning. They wanted to get as much done as possible because they wouldn't be able to return next week. The harvest festival would eat up their whole day. When Micah had explained this to Reuben a couple of days ago, the bishop had accepted the delay.

"All things happen in God's time," Reuben said, "including harvest festivals." His grin had been bright through his gray whiskers. "Enjoy yourself with your friend and his family. The panels will be done when they're done."

The bishop's generous words and kind smile had added to Micah's guilt at not mentioning one important fact—Katie Kay would be going to the harvest festival with him and the Donnellys.

This morning, his stomach had twisted around and around on the drive over in his buggy to meet Sean at the Lapps' house. Facing Reuben and not being able to tell his bishop the truth about Katie Kay had kept him awake most of the night. The fear Sean might accidentally mention Reuben's daughter had prevented him from sleeping the rest of the night.

He'd been able to breathe a bit easier when he discovered Reuben was visiting a family in his other district and would be gone most of the day. Before Sean arrived with their equipment, Micah had spent a few minutes speaking with Marnita and Ina Sue, Katie Kay's two younger sisters. They were excited about the young people's singing planned for the following evening and talked of nothing else.

It was odd to think that not long ago, he anticipated youth events with the same eagerness. That time, which was simple in retrospect, seemed like someone else's life.

Once he had climbed onto the roof with his partner, Micah had tried to lose himself in his work. Instead he kept losing the bolts and nuts he need to assemble the framework.

Looking over at Sean, he asked, "Do you have more of those small bolts? I'm out."

"That makes two of us," Sean said after checking the pockets of his work apron. "Guess it's time to run over to the hardware store and replenish the supplies. I should have gone yesterday after work, but our house guest made her delicious chocolate cake and I didn't want to risk having it all eaten by three kids and one pregnant wife before I got home." He bent and gave a gentle tug on the framework. "It's not going anywhere. We'll get back to it next weekend."

"Ja." He was accustomed to his partner stating the obvious. Shortly after they'd begun working together,

Micah realized that talking aloud was Sean's way of reviewing the next steps on a project.

After they'd collected their tools and climbed down, Sean carried a length of the metal framework to the van. They'd need it to make sure they got the right-sized bolts. Micah followed, pausing to let Reuben's daughters know he and Sean were done for the day.

"We'll be back the Saturday after next to finish the work," he said, though Reuben knew already.

"*Danki*, Micah." Ina Sue, who must be almost twenty, smiled at him. "You're nice to do this for *Daed* and for us."

"Sean is helping, too." He sounded idiotic, but he hadn't expected Katie Kay's sister to regard him with an invitation to linger.

"Will you be at the singing tomorrow night?"

"I don't think so." Most of the kids who joined in the youth events were too young for him. The guys were interested in pushing the envelope of their plain lives and trying to get a girl to drive home. A few had jobs beyond their family farms, but they hadn't decided what to do with their lives.

Telling the girls he'd see them at church in the morning, he strode to the van. He was walking a narrow line between his Amish life and the *Englisch* world where he worked. Every step had to be made with care.

Did Katie Kay feel that way, too? Or was she more comfortable among the *Englischers*? She continued to wear *Englisch* clothing but had begun to cover her head when she was doing housework. Was it a sign she was considering a return to her family? He'd heard her telling Sean's *kinder* about the school she and Micah had attended. The wistfulness in her voice had given him hope, but he cautioned himself not to be overly optimistic. She might not intend to resume her life among their people.

Micah was glad that, while they drove to Sean's house, they made a list of items they'd use the following week for the work on Reuben's house. He wrote down each part and the quantity they needed, adding in the ones he thought of while Sean called out others. Focusing kept him from thinking about Katie Kay.

For a few seconds anyhow.

As they entered the house, he heard the rumble of the vacuum. The kids came running, and the loud noise turned off. While Sean greeted his *kinder*, Micah watched Katie Kay lean the vacuum against a chair.

She went to the sofa and assisted Gemma to her feet. Gemma put her hand to her side, grimacing, but her smile returned while she thanked Katie Kay.

Waddling to the entry hall, one hand under her distended belly, Gemma asked, "What's brought you home early, Sean? Not that I'm complaining."

"We've got to run to the hardware store for some parts. I wanted to see if you needed anything from Strasburg while we're over that way."

"Pumpkins!" shouted DJ.

"Let Mommy answer." Sean gave his eldest a chiding frown.

DJ wasn't cowed. "But, Daddy, you promised to take us to get pumpkins the next time you went to the hardware store. Big, medium and small."

When Micah saw Katie Kay's confusion, he said, "Sean started a tradition a few years ago of making pumpkin people. Because the cold can cause Olivia to have an asthma attack, she can't build snowmen. They solved the problem and got a jump on the cold weather with pumpkin people. They use carrots for noses, though a hole has to be carved out to fit the carrot in. The kids help set them up and then they paint clothes and faces on them out in the front yard."

"With the paint they don't splash on themselves," Gemma added with a tired smile.

"Can we go?" asked the *kinder* in unison.

Micah smiled at how the Donnelly kids could be of one mind when they wanted something.

Sean hesitated. "I know I promised, but Mommy is tired."

"I can go," Katie Kay piped up. "Micah and I will help to keep an eye on them while they pick out their pumpkins. That makes one *kind* for each adult. It should be simple." She glanced at Micah. "Ain't so?"

He nodded because he could see how exhausted Gemma was. Having the kids whining because of a broken promise would upset her. She needed her rest and peace and quiet.

"Thank you." Gemma's grateful smile was aimed at them. "I think I will—"

"You will sit and watch TV or take a nap." Katie Kay put her hands on the other woman's shoulders and steered her to the couch. "While Sean and Micah help the kids get their coats on, I'll make you a cup of herbal tea to sip on while we're away."

"But supper—"

Again Katie Kay interrupted. "Don't worry about that. I'll take care of it later. Enjoy your quiet time. You know it won't last long."

Micah said nothing as Gemma nodded, her every motion heavy with fatigue. She trusted Katie Kay with her *kinder*. The two women had grown closer as they spent more time together. He was tempted to ask

Gemma how that had happened. Every attempt he made to heal the wounds between him and Katie Kay failed.

Because you keep pressuring her to make a decision instead of letting her find the way with God's help.

He was getting really annoyed with his conscience. At the same time, he had to be grateful for its guidance. It hadn't steered him wrong in the past, so he should heed it now.

Helping three small *kinder* into their coats was like trying to capture newborn piglets. They wiggled and jostled and reached in front of one another to collect hats. Three *kinder* seemed like a dozen. Micah wasn't surprised that Katie Kay had already returned from the kitchen with a cup of steaming tea by the time they finished getting the youngsters dressed.

When Jayden announced he needed to go to the bathroom, she took his hand and motioned for Micah and Sean to take his siblings out.

"We'll be there before you get them strapped in," she said, leading the little boy to the downstairs bathroom.

Micah had no doubts about that. DJ and Olivia ran in circles around him and Sean as they went outside. They bounced like a pair of rabbits and asked questions without giving him or Sean a chance to answer.

"We'll take Gemma's van." Sean grinned. "It's easier than moving their car seats. I already put the structure piece from Reuben's house in the back. Do you have our list, Micah?"

"I'll get it." He strode to the work van and opened the passenger door. His clipboard had fallen on the floor, so he shook dirt off it as he returned to the other vehicle.

He was glad, when he got back, that Katie Kay was sitting with the *kinder* and helping Jayden into his car seat. The ancient Volkswagen microbus had a bench seat in the front with seat belts for three adults. Sitting next to Katie Kay during the ride to the hardware store would be exquisite torture.

His fingers itched to caress her cheek, which he knew was silken-soft. His arm ached to curve around her shoulders as it had when he'd drawn her to him in his courting buggy. His senses recalled the sweet scent of her shampoo.

Micah forced the memories away as he climbed into the front seat and didn't turn to look at her and the *kinder*. Whenever he remembered what he and Katie Kay had shared—for such a brief moment—in the past, he couldn't imagine a future without her.

Though she'd given him no sign she felt the same.

Fool!

That was what he was. The biggest *dummkopf* ever.

Yet, knowing that, why couldn't he put her out of his mind? He needed to find an answer right away.

The hardware store in Strasburg was set behind its narrow parking lot. Unlike the fancy outlet mall on the Lincoln Highway in Ronks or the shops in Intercourse and Bird-in-Hand, this store focused on service for local farmers rather than tourists. A large sign painted Hardware was set atop the roof of the front porch running the length of the building. On the concrete floor was a variety of items, some on sale and others, seasonal clearance. Dried cornstalks were stacked on either side of the door, and pumpkins were heaped beneath a lean-to shed to the far left side of the building. A pair of horses waited with their plain buggies near a hitching rail.

Micah was glad to hear Katie Kay insist that each of the *kinder* must hold a grown-up's hand before they started across the almost empty parking lot. Cars and trucks often zipped in and out.

It took about five minutes—far less time than Micah had expected—for the *kinder* to pick out the pumpkins they wanted. Sean lifted their choices onto a flatbed cart. He let his *kinder* "help" pull the cart toward the outside register, where they paid for nine pumpkins.

After putting the pumpkins into the van, they went into the store to look for the parts they needed. Sean asked Micah to help Katie Kay with the youngsters.

"I will get what we need," Sean said with a grin. "And I'll do it much faster without small fingers exploring what's in the bins."

Something about how his partner's eyes twinkled warned Micah that Sean had an ulterior motive for sending him with Katie Kay and the *kinder*. He was tempted to tell Sean that matchmaking could undermine their friendship, but he knew it wouldn't. And Micah couldn't be certain that leaving him with Katie Kay was Sean's primary motivation, especially when they were chaperoned by three imps who demanded all their attention.

After nodding to Sean, Micah looked at the kids. "What shall we look at first?"

"Need paint! For our pumpkin people," announced DJ. "Black paint."

"And white," added Olivia.

Jayden refused to be left out. "And bluenette."

"Bluenette?" Micah asked.

"For a pumpkin lady's hair."

Micah remained puzzled until Katie Kay whispered, "I think he means *brunette*."

He had to pretend to cough so he didn't laugh as they walked along an aisle. Jayden selected a small can of paint with a bright blue lid and announced he was painting his pumpkin lady with bluenette hair. Arching a brow at Katie Kay, Micah took the can from the little boy.

"Bluenette, it is," Micah said as he collected the white and black cans from the other two *kinder*. "Let's go and pay for these."

He had taken two steps when he realized Katie Kay wasn't following. Did she need something else? He couldn't imagine what she might be shopping for at a hardware store. Turning around, he was astonished to see her holding on to a shelf, her face as gray as the labels on the paint cans beside her.

"Are you okay?" he asked.

"Shhh!" She put her finger to her lips.

He raised his brows in a silent question.

"It's your brother," she whispered.

"Which one?"

"Your *twin* brother."

"Are you sure?"

"*Ja*. Daniel looks just like you."

Micah frowned. He should have remembered that coming with Katie Kay close to Strasburg was a risk. For the past six months, Daniel had been overseeing a massive project on a farm outside the village. His brother was a skilled carpenter, but he'd been challenged since he was hired by an *Englischer* to repair an old stone-end farmhouse and its half dozen outbuildings. As Daniel had said more than once, the only thing holding up the structures were the termites.

He wanted to ask Katie Kay if she was sure about what she'd seen; then he heard Daniel's laugh and the low rumble of his brother's voice that others told him were much like his own. Hoping both he and Katie

Kay were wrong, he peered around the end of the row to confirm their suspicions.

Daniel was talking to the store manager at the rear of the store. He couldn't have seen Micah or any of them. So far, so *gut*.

Micah said in not much more than a whisper, "I'll distract him while you slip out the door. Get in the van and keep yourself and the *kinder* out of sight until I join you."

She nodded, and he realized how distraught she was. Shrinking along the aisle and drawing Sean's kids with her, she motioned for him to hurry.

Micah hoped she'd be sensible. He almost laughed aloud at the thought. If she'd done the sensible thing and gone home, she wouldn't have to skulk through the store. Maybe this encounter would persuade her to reunite with her family.

As if he didn't have a care in the world, Micah sauntered around the end of the aisle. He set the three cans of paint on the counter and greeted his brother.

Daniel grinned. "What are you doing down here? I thought you were working on Reuben's house today."

"We are, but we needed to stock up on a few things." He glanced into the basket his brother carried. "More drywall screws? I thought you had the walls up."

"In the main house. Mrs. O'Neill has decided she wants to use the old stable as a guesthouse, though there are five guest rooms in the big house."

Micah congratulated himself on changing the subject. It was his brother's first large project as a general contractor, and Daniel was enjoying every minute of being his own boss, a goal he'd set for himself when they were teens.

Trying not to be obvious, Micah glanced toward the

front door several times. Why hadn't Katie Kay slipped out yet? He could keep his brother chatting, but eventually Sean would be done.

His brother stopped in the middle of a word and looked past him. "Did you see her?"

"Her?" He was glad Daniel wasn't looking at him, because he guessed his face revealed his anxiety.

"By the front door."

Micah turned around, holding his breath as he prayed he wouldn't see Katie Kay at the door. When an elderly man walked into the store, he looked at his brother. "Have you thought about getting glasses? That guy doesn't look like a *her.*"

"Not him. A woman just left. She looked a lot like... Okay, you're going to find this strange. She looked a lot like Katie Kay Lapp."

"Did she?" Micah wouldn't lie to his twin brother. If Daniel asked him if he'd seen Katie Kay, he'd give his brother an honest answer. "I didn't notice any plain women in here."

"She didn't look plain. She looked like Katie Kay would if she were *Englisch.*" He grinned. "Maybe I do need glasses. What would she be doing here?"

"Who knows?"

"I sure don't." His smile widened. "You dodged a bullet there."

"*Dodged a bullet*? Where did you learn that saying?"

Daniel's grin became a laugh. "Believe or not, from *Grossmammi* Ella. She learned it from one of the therapists who help her hold on to what memory she has left. For someone who has trouble recalling names, she can remember bizarre phrases and uses them over and over until the rest of us pick them up."

"How's she doing?" Micah was again relieved that

Katie Kay was no longer the subject. *Grossmammi* Ella was the great-grandmother of Daniel's fiancée, Hannah, and Daniel had a great deal of affection for the cantankerous, headstrong old woman who sometimes, while lost in her memories, believed he was her late husband.

"Better than we thought a few months ago. The memory exercises she's doing seems to be stabilizing her Alzheimer's. We know it's not a long-term solution, but we count each day she's able to recognize us a blessing."

Micah paid for the paint and then stepped aside to let Daniel check out. When Sean walked toward them, Micah waved him back. Renewed guilt bore into him, and he knew only one way to ease it.

Katie Kay needed to go home, and he had to help her see that. He prayed God would send inspiration to show him how.

If the *kinder* thought she'd lost her mind as she hurried them to the van and helped them in, Katie Kay didn't try to persuade them otherwise. Instead she made a game out of keeping hidden in the van. She heard them whispering together about surprising their *daed* and Micah with cries of "Boo!"

Daniel's buggy was on the other side of the parking lot, and he wouldn't hear the *kinder* from there. He might, however, notice the little ones moving about the van, so she devised excuse after excuse, each one sillier than the one before, for them to crouch between the seats.

"I want to see my pumpkins," DJ announced, a sign he was bored with the game. He started to scramble over the seat as the unmistakable sound of metal buggy wheels and iron horseshoes sounded on the asphalt.

She grabbed the little boy by the heels and pulled

him down beside the rest of them on the floor. Before he could protest loudly enough to be heard outside the van, she began making goofy faces at the three *kinder* and dared them to do the same. As they distorted their features into every possible shape, they laughed. She kept up the game until she knew the buggy must be gone.

Looking out, she saw Micah and Sean walking toward them. She started to get up, but this time the *kinder* reminded her to stay out of sight because they wanted to "scare" their *daed* and Micah. As she joined in with their game, she wondered how much longer she could avoid making the inevitable decisions about going home…and about Micah.

Gemma was asleep on the sofa when Katie Kay walked into the living room. Before she could ask the little ones to be quiet, they ran to their *mamm* and began chattering about the pumpkins they'd found. Half-asleep, Gemma gathered them to her and listened to their excitement, though her face was pale and she winced when she sat.

"Stay where you are," Katie Kay urged. Looking over her shoulder, she added, "Sean, sit and enjoy your family while Micah and I make supper."

"I don't cook," Micah protested.

She laughed at his shock at doing what was considered among the Amish women's work. "Then it's time you learn. With Wanda getting married soon, you may be on your own to prepare your supper."

"Leah usually—"

"*Ja*, I know you depend on your sister-in-law to cook for you when you're not eating here. However, it won't hurt you to flip grilled cheese sandwiches while I make soup."

Sean grinned as he took the bag of paint cans from Micah. "She's got you there, my friend. I think your masculinity will survive giving her a hand making one meal."

"You're no help," Micah tossed back but grinned. "Show me what you need me to do, Katie Kay."

In the kitchen, she was pleased to discover he wasn't as inept as he'd complained. He followed her directions and got bread out of the drawer, as well as butter and cheese from the fridge. Spreading the ingredients across the table, he left her the small area by the stove to cut vegetables into a soup she was making with leftover chicken from earlier in the week.

Neither of them spoke of her near encounter with his twin brother at the hardware store. She wondered if he was relieved to focus on cooking and let everything else go. She was, because she could talk and laugh with him without having any of the issues plaguing them intrude.

During supper, Katie Kay enjoyed the calm within herself. She had to make decisions but not at that moment. She listened as the three youngsters told their *mamm*—again—about their trip to the hardware store and their plans for the pumpkins. Gemma's lips twitched at Jayden's intention to paint "bluenette" hair on his pumpkin person tomorrow after church. He didn't notice because he was excited. It would be his first time to help with the painting.

Katie Kay, along with Sean and Micah, insisted Gemma rest after the meal. When Micah offered to help clean up, Katie Kay was pleased. It was lonely in the kitchen while she listened to the family enjoying each other's company in the living room.

Taking the plates and bowls from the table, Katie Kay set them on the counter. She frowned at the solidified cheese sticking to the top one. It needed to be removed before it could be washed.

"I'll scrape," she said, "if you'll load the dishwasher, Micah. You do know how to do that, don't you?"

"Gemma taught me long ago."

She chuckled as she handed him the first plate, and he put it in the proper part of the dishwasher. As they were finishing, Olivia ran in and gave her a hug. Jayden did the same. She wished them a *gut nacht*, which made them giggle as they did whenever she used *Deitsch*. She edged aside as they embraced Micah and ran back into the living room. Hearing the Donnellys heading upstairs to put the *kinder* to bed, she reached for another plate.

"The kids like you," Micah said.

"They are sweet and funny."

"I wasn't sure at first if you liked *kinder*."

She halted with the final plate held over the trash can. Setting it on a nearby counter, she asked, "What gave you that idea?"

"You never offered to watch the little ones during church services."

"I spent every waking hour, except those few at church every other week, taking care of my younger sisters. To be able to sit and listen to God's word and not have to worry about someone sticking a finger into the washer's wringer or trying to see the bottom of the well was *wunderbaar*."

Resting his hand on the counter, he faced her. "I didn't realize that."

"I know. I didn't want to shame *Daed* by whining."

"Why not? All of us kids complained about our chores at one time or another."

"But you weren't the bishop's *kind*. We're held to

a higher standard so other *kinder* can strive to do as we did."

When he didn't reply, she finished the plate. She handed it to him along with the rinsed bowls. He put them into the dishwasher.

As he snapped the door shut, he said, "I guess I should have known how it would be for you, but I never thought about it."

"It was all we were allowed to think about." She didn't add that Priscilla had mentioned the need for them to be role models at least once a day before she married. After that, her older sister had repeated the words each time she arrived for a visit and every time on her way out the door.

"Can I tell you something I've been wondering about?" he asked.

"What?"

"Something that isn't any of my business."

She sat at the table and looked at him with a grimace. "Which means it's something to do with me and the *boppli*."

"How did you guess?"

"Because you act as if you're tiptoeing through a rattlesnake nest whenever you want to talk about the *boppli*."

He pulled out the chair next to hers and moved it so their knees were only an inch from each other. Abruptly she was aware of him as she hadn't been since they walked out together. No, that wasn't true. She was always vividly connected to his voice, where his hands were, what he was looking at. It was the only way she could keep the barriers up between him and her heart, which teased her to reconsider what she'd said to him when she'd ended their relationship, not guessing then that she also had rung a death knell over their friendship.

When he took her hands and folded them between his, she was so stunned she didn't jerk them back. And then it was too late because the heat seeping from his fingers to hers was delightful, and she didn't want to put an end to it.

Ice froze her next breath when he said, "I've been pondering this question for a while. Do you intend to keep your *kind*, or are you planning to give it up for adoption?"

Words vanished from Katie Kay's mind. Usually she had a quick answer for any question, whether it was a gentle word for a *kind* or a scathing one for someone who annoyed her. Now she couldn't come up with anything to say as he asked about the subject she'd avoided thinking about.

"I haven't decided what I'll do when the time comes." That was the truth.

He sighed with relief. "I'm glad to hear that because I thought you had."

"Why?"

"You say *the boppli*, never *my boppli*."

Did she? She hadn't noticed that. Was it a habit, or did the choice of words have a deeper meaning? She cringed when anyone mentioned the *boppli* was Austin's, whether she was among *Englischers* or the Amish. But she hadn't realized she never spoke of the *kind* growing within her as hers.

"I've been praying for guidance," she said softly.

"You have?"

"Why do you sound surprised? I didn't leave Paradise Springs because I wanted to get away from God."

"Then why did you leave?"

For a moment, she considered giving him the same excuse she'd used whenever anyone asked her the question. She'd been honest with him. Why not continue?

"I needed to see what else the world had to share with me. I left because I felt caged."

It was his turn to be speechless. She took advantage of his astonishment to slip her hands from between his and hurry out of the kitchen before he could ask another question that made her face what could become a bleak future.

Chapter Ten

The following Saturday, Katie Kay sat between Olivia and Jayden on the rearmost seat of Gemma's van. As he'd promised the Donnellys, Micah had pounded out the small dent in the front bumper. Only a few dark spots on the bright chrome remained as a reminder of the damage.

She wished she could pay for the chrome paint. She'd seen what the small cans cost at the hardware store. Her plan had been to select one and ask Micah to buy it. She'd reimburse him when she could. That, along with giving Gemma a break, was why she'd gone to the hardware store, but all her plans had gone out the window when she'd seen Daniel Stoltzfus. All she'd thought about then was slipping away without being noticed.

Her heart beat double time whenever she thought of how close discovery had been. If Micah hadn't assisted her by distracting his twin brother, she wouldn't have been able to get out of the hardware store unobserved. She was thankful for that.

But her heart pounded harder when she thought about holding hands with Micah in the Donnellys' kitchen. When they were walking out, she'd been overwhelmed by the intense attraction between them, but the memory of the few times he'd taken her hand then seemed to pale in comparison with the powerful sensations that had swept through her while they sat facing each other.

Today she was also grateful the two *kinder* had pleaded for her to join them at the back of the van. Their request allowed her to avoid going through the awkward motions of not sitting beside Micah and DJ on the middle bench. She could have insisted on riding in the front with Sean and Gemma, but it would have been crowded with three adults—one of them *very* pregnant—on the bench seat.

She hoped she wouldn't get carsick. She had once while riding in the back seat of Vinnie's car, but he'd been making wild turns from one of Lancaster's streets to another, laughing when the rear end slid and the tires squealed. He hadn't wanted to stop until he realized she was serious she was about to throw up. He'd pulled over just in time for her to get out of the car and be sick on the curb.

It didn't seem to be a problem with Sean behind the wheel. She couldn't help noticing how much more smoothly he shifted the vehicle than she had. It didn't bounce like a jackrabbit as it had when she tried to downshift the first few times on the way to Lancaster.

When they arrived almost an hour later at the farm where the harvest festival was being held, traffic was backed up for more than a mile. Ahead of them, cars drove through an open gate into a field past the stone farmhouse and the circular red barn decorated with Pennsylvania Dutch symbols she'd heard called hex signs. She'd been asked about them while she lived in Lancaster, and each time she'd said she didn't know anything about them. She wasn't surprised by the questions because many people assumed the terms *Pennsylvania Dutch* and *the Amish* were identical. The Amish were one group among the many German speakers who'd settled in southeastern Pennsylvania in the eighteenth century.

Olivia and Jayden, like their older brother, peered out the windows as the van inched forward. Finally it was their turn to edge onto the dirt road leading to a man wearing a bright yellow vest and holding a baton with a red flag at the end, who motioned them toward a long row of parked cars.

The kids laughed as the old van bounced on the uneven ground.

"Ouch!" groaned Micah when the wheels hit a deeper rut. He rubbed his head, and the *kinder* giggled. He gave them a fake scowl, which made them laugh harder when he asked, "Do you think it's funny my hat might be cracked?"

"As long as it's not your head," called Sean as he parked the van between two pickup trucks. "If that hit the roof, you might punch a hole right through it with your hard head."

Katie Kay joined in with the laughter as she helped Olivia and Jayden loosen the seat belts woven through their car seats. Another item she needed to get before the *boppli* was born. She suspected they were very expensive.

You won't need one if you go home, her conscience reminded her. Amish women usually carried their *bopplin* in their arms when someone else was driving the buggy. If she were driving it herself, she could keep the *boppli* on her lap or make a nest of blankets and quilts on the floor to keep the little one safe.

She nodded her thanks when Micah offered his hand

to help her from the van. Then she released it so she could lift the younger two Donnelly *kinder* out. The little ones acted as if they'd replaced their bones with bedsprings; they bounced around the adults, unable to restrain their excitement. She understood how they felt, because a thrill of anticipation raced through her, too.

Families and groups of teenagers walked between the rows of parked cars, and everyone seemed as eager as the Donnelly kids. Everyone was chatting and laughing, and Katie Kay let those *gut* spirits wash over her like a cleansing rain. Today was for having fun, something she didn't want to forget how to have.

Aromas of fried dough and hot dogs, as well as peppers and onions, welcomed them into the festival's midway. Booths lined either side of the wide walkway, where the grass had been ground into the dirt. At each one, *kinder* waited for their opportunity to win a prize.

However, DJ, Olivia and Jayden had one destination in mind. They wanted to take a hayride, especially Jayden who'd been too young last year to go. Until they did that, they weren't interested in anything else, though Micah whispered he'd prefer to wait until he could get a sausage sandwich with those delicious onions and peppers.

When they reached the field where the hayrides were under way, a hand-painted sign announced rides were available, first-come, first-served. The teenage girl selling tickets leaned her elbow on one of the uprights, looking bored.

Gemma exchanged a glance with her husband, and Katie Kay knew she shouldn't try to catch its meaning. It was, however, obvious. Gemma wanted to let the *kinder* ride, but she didn't feel *gut* enough.

"We'll take them," Katie Kay said, cutting her eyes

toward Micah. "That way, you two can rest and have something to eat. And get Micah a sausage sandwich before he fades away from hunger."

"You don't have to do that." Gemma's protests were halfhearted.

"We'd be glad to do it." She turned to Micah and asked, "Aren't we?"

She was glad when he didn't hesitate. "*Ja*. C'mon, kids. Let's get in line so we can take our turn."

"A sandwich will be waiting for you," Sean said, laughing. "What about for you, Katie Kay? Do you want one, too?"

"No," Micah answered before she could. "Katie Kay will want fried dough with plenty of powdered sugar and cinnamon on it." He smiled at her. "Ain't so?"

"*Ja*. How did you know?"

"I heard your stomach rumble when we walked by. It's true actions speak louder than words." He laughed, and the kids did, too, as if it were the funniest thing they'd ever heard.

Sean gave a feigned groan. "You see what I have to put up with every day."

As Gemma checked to make sure each *kind* had his or her coat buttoned, Katie Kay looked at the man beside her.

Micah was grinning as widely as the youngsters. He was a *gut* friend to the Donnellys. She wished she could say he was her friend, too. Or did she? Was friendship all she wanted with him?

The question unsettled her, and she pushed it away. She didn't want to think about such things while they were at the festival. She wanted to have fun.

"*Danki*, Micah," Katie Kay said as they walked toward the girl who was selling tickets to an *Englisch* family. "I know riding around on a flatbed wagon isn't a big treat for someone who grew up on a farm."

"You grew up on a farm, too."

"*Ja*, but…" How could she explain to him that in her few months away from the countryside she'd missed the open fields and the cool sensation of freshly turned earth between her toes and the rich scents of plants and animals and a *snitz* pie cooling on a windowsill? More than once, she'd considered leaving Lancaster just to rediscover what she'd left behind. If she had, she might not be pregnant.

She refused to think that way. She wanted to enjoy the day with the *kinder*, their parents…and Micah. Today was for happiness and fun. Trouble would return soon enough.

As they reached the front of the line and Katie Kay began helping the two littlest ones onto the wagon, Sean pulled Micah aside and said, "Thanks for taking the kids." He'd already said it a half-dozen times. He must have been really worried about Gemma getting overtired. As Katie Kay had, his partner said, "I know riding around on a horse-drawn farm wagon isn't a big treat for you, but it is for my kids."

"Riding around on a horse-drawn farm wagon and not having to spend the whole day sweating out in the field *is* a big treat for me." He laughed and was glad when Sean joined in.

Micah bent to hoist DJ up but paused long enough to sneak a glance at Sean, who had his arm around Gemma. Sean was worried about his pregnant wife. A flush of something that felt like sorrow flowed through him. Katie Kay wouldn't have anyone to be concerned for her when she was as rotund as Gemma. The *daed* of her *boppli* had cut any ties with her in the cruelest possible ways. Nobody would stand beside her as Sean did with Gemma, encouraging her and celebrating the new life with her. She alone would have to choose her *boppli*'s name.

He tried not to think of that as he put his hands on Katie Kay's still slender waist and lifted her to sit beside DJ. Climbing on himself, he pointed to one of the bales in the center. "You boys sit here, and, Olivia, you sit—"

"With Kay-Kay," the little girl announced as she settled herself on one of the bales and patted the hay. "Come and sit with me, Kay-Kay."

"How could I resist such an invitation?" She sat beside the *kind* and put her arm around Olivia's narrow shoulders. "You will hold on to me so I don't fall off the wagon, won't you?"

The little girl nodded so hard her braids bounced like a pair of reins along her back.

Though the ride was around an open field with the horses plodding at a pace barely faster than the *kinder* could walk, the Donnelly youngsters were thrilled with the experience. They talked without seeming to take a breath.

Micah relaxed and listened as they discussed the wagon, the horses and the harvest festival in specific detail. Now that they were enjoying their ride, their next thoughts were for lunch.

Or the boys' thoughts were.

Olivia was absorbed with a different matter. "I needs a bonnet. Girls on TV have bonnets."

"Which girls?" Katie Kay asked.

The little girl began to chatter about a show about a family that lived on the prairie. "They wears bonnets when they ride in a wagon. Mommy says girls always wears bonnets long ago."

"That's true," she replied as if the matter was the most serious one in the world.

Olivia pointed to the line, where others waited for their turn to get on the wagon. "See? They gots pretty bonnets."

Instantly Katie Kay stiffened. He could read her thoughts as if she spoke them aloud: Were there Amish at the festival? She should have known that they could encounter plain people there.

He scanned the line again and smiled. The girls in the blue-and-white-checked bonnets were *Englisch*.

"I see," she said to Olivia, and he noticed her shoulders relax.

"I wants a bonnet." The *kind* looked up at Katie Kay with innocent eyes. "Where can I gets a bonnet?"

Katie Kay glanced at Micah. He shrugged. He had no idea where an *Englisch* girl would obtain a checkered bonnet. Were they sold in stores, or were the brightly colored bonnets homemade? *Mamm* had made the far simpler bonnets she and his sisters wore.

"Where's your bonnet, Kay-Kay?" asked Olivia, obviously not ready to let the subject drop. "Uncle Micah says Amish girls wear bonnets to school and to church. You're Amish, aren't you?"

He waited to see how Katie Kay would answer. Did she still consider herself Amish? She used *Deitsch* words often and wore a kerchief over her hair when she worked around the house. But both might be habit more than anything.

"Ja," she replied with a smile. "Amish girls do wear bonnets to school and church."

Olivia wasn't satisfied with Katie Kay's evasion, and

neither was Micah. He listened as the little girl asked again, "So where's your bonnet, Kay-Kay?"

"At my *daed*'s house." Katie Kay started to add more, but Olivia sneezed once, then a second, then a third time.

"Gesundheit," he and Katie Kay said at the same time.

The youngsters giggled, and they began to talk again about the horses pulling the wagon. Micah wished he could figure out a way to return the conversation to bonnets and ask if Katie Kay planned to wear hers again.

He wondered if she'd finally faced the future and had made up her mind about what she intended to do with the *boppli*. Surrendering a *kind* was unusual in the Amish community, but it happened. A family beyond the biological parents' districts would be found for the little one. It would be adopted by a plain couple who would love it as if the *boppli* had been born within that family. But the choice had to be Katie Kay's.

The only decision he needed to make was if he wanted to sample at least once more the delight he'd rediscovered when he held her hands last night. His aim had been to offer her comfort while he posed such difficult questions. Then pleasure had skittered up his arm, and he'd found himself wanting to look into her eyes for the rest of his life.

Be careful, he warned himself as the wagon completed its circuit. He jumped off. Helping the others down, he thought about the *Englisch* saying Sean used often with a laugh. What was it?

Fool me once, shame on you. Fool me twice, shame on me.

That was the one, but he didn't feel the least bit like laughing. If he let himself be taken in by Katie Kay again, the resulting pain in his heart would be his own fault.

The boys ran to the gate where Sean and Gemma waited. Olivia sneezed again and again. Was she allergic to hay? It seemed unlikely because there were fields on every side of the Donnellys' house. Katie Kay gave the little girl a tissue so she could blow her nose.

"She may be getting a cold," Gemma said as they walked toward the midway. "I hope not. Once one gets sick, they all do."

"At least you don't have as many *kinder* as in my family." Micah chuckled. "*Mamm* used to dose each of us as soon as one got sick. We'd catch the cold or whatever but not as hard."

"A good idea." Gemma hooked her arm through her husband's. "Sean, I do believe you owe Micah a sausage sandwich."

They laughed as they picked out what they wanted for lunch and found a picnic table to enjoy it while they watched the other festivalgoers. Micah listened to the *kinder* plan what they wanted to do after they ate. A single glance at Gemma told him she hoped to sit at the table for as long as possible. The only way she'd do that was if he and Katie Kay amused the youngsters.

"What do you think about doing the corn maze?" he asked her softly enough so the chattering *kinder* wouldn't overhear.

"I've never done a corn maze. Have you?"

He shook his head. "But I've been curious about them. It's got to take a lot of skill to carve a cornfield into a pattern that looks like a giant table with a turkey dinner spread across it."

"A pattern?"

Pulling out the pamphlet he'd taken from a stack

near the parking lot, he opened it. "See? This is what the maze looks like from overhead."

"It is a turkey!" Olivia cried as she peeked over his arm and poked the page. "Mommy, can we do the turkey?"

Gemma said, "I don't know. That's a long walk."

"We'll take them if you'd like," Katie Kay said. "I know you want to spend time with them, too, but if you'd prefer to relax, we'll take them through the maze."

"And get them tired out." Micah winked at Gemma. "That way, they'll go to sleep right away when they get home."

"That sounds lovely," she said before looking at her husband. "Sean?"

"If Micah and Katie Kay want to wrangle three scamps through the maze, I say go for it."

Micah nodded as he saw Sean's thankful expression. "It's a deal. Just make sure you have plenty of fried dough—"

"And popcorn," added Jayden.

"And popcorn," he repeated with a smile. "According to the brochure, it takes on average a little over an hour to complete the maze."

"A feast will be waiting upon your return from vanquishing yon corn maze," Sean said so seriously they laughed.

Leading the kids and Katie Kay, Micah went to the booth to buy tickets for them. They were asked to wait to the left of the entrance, because guests were spaced out to make it impossible to follow someone else around the twisting maze.

When it was their turn to go in, the man at the entrance said, "Have fun. When you smell pumpkin pie, you will be right close to the exit."

Olivia giggled and grabbed Micah's hand and then Katie Kay's. DJ took his other hand while Katie Kay offered hers to Jayden. Together, they entered the maze.

Around them, the dried corn leaves rustled with the slight breeze they had hardly noticed before. The kids stared around, wide-eyed, but giggled at each other's trepidation. The ground was well worn under their feet. Voices, disembodied and distorted by the stalks, reached them in snippets.

The kids asked to go ahead to the first intersection of the paths. Agreeing not to turn in any direction until the adults reached them, they skipped away. Olivia stopped to sneeze twice and then cough, but she shook her head when he asked if she needed her asthma medicine. She hurried after her brothers.

"Do you have her inhaler, Micah?" Katie Kay asked.

"No." Dismay shot through him. "I forgot to get it from Gemma."

"Then we should hurry. Maybe her coughing is nothing, but I don't want her to have an attack."

He nodded and matched her steps as they followed the *kinder.*

"While they're out of earshot," Micah said, "I wanted to tell you, Katie Kay, I'm sorry for pressuring you. When you called your little one 'the *boppli,*' I thought you'd already made up your mind about what you would do with him or her."

"I haven't. I don't want to. Not yet. Can you understand that?"

"Ja." He smiled at her as they went together to where the *kinder* waited impatiently.

She conferred with them about which direction they should choose. They decided to go left and ran toward the next intersection, where people could be seen walking both ways. The five of them kept to the same pattern over and over with the *kinder* racing to the turn ahead of them, sometimes reaching a dead end and having to turn around.

As they retraced their steps a second time back to a branch of the maze, Micah reached out for the *kinder*'s hands, but when his fingers closed around slender fingers, he knew he hadn't caught either Olivia or DJ. Instead he was holding Katie Kay's hand.

Drop it! The warning was like a fire siren blaring through his head, but he couldn't make his fingers uncurl from around hers. Not even when other people going through the maze edged around where they stood in the middle of the path.

Drop it!

He couldn't. He'd waited for the chance to hold her hand again. As he did, the months since the last time he'd taken her home from a singing melted away like frost on a sunny morning.

When she raised her eyes to meet his, he couldn't mistake her expression. She was as pleased and as uneasy as he was. In spite of that, she didn't tug her hand away.

He drew her to the side of the path, stopping though the kids waved for them to catch up. The sharp edges of a corn leaf brushed against his ear, and he edged a single step away.

"This is the most fun I've had in a long time," he said.

"The kids are excited, and that's fun."

"Being here with you is fun for me." He ran his thumb along her palm. "I've missed our friendship."

"Me, too." She squeezed his fingers as her smile grew soft. As soft as her lips would be, he knew.

His rebellious heart leaped within his chest. He'd never wanted to kiss her—not even the first time—as much as he did now. Would friendship be enough for him with this woman he'd once loved?

An hour passed and then a second one, and yet Katie Kay remained lost with Micah and the *kinder* in the maze. She wouldn't have worried except that Olivia coughed more. Was it a cold, or was she having an asthma attack? Olivia seemed to be breathing okay, but Katie Kay wasn't sure how an attack progressed. She knew Micah was apprehensive about the little girl's situation, too, because he picked the *kind* up and carried her when she lagged.

Katie Kay did the same with Jayden. DJ was no longer running ahead, and he complained on every step he was thirsty, though he'd had a full bottle of water when they entered the maze.

When they reached what seemed like the thousandth intersection in the maze, Micah pointed to the right. "I think we're supposed to go that way."

"No, this way," DJ argued, gesturing left.

"Why do you think so?"

"I've seen a bunch of people go that way, and I haven't seen them backtrack."

"That's *gut* enough for me." He held out his hand, but she gave DJ a gentle shove in Micah's direction. The little boy grasped his fingers and began to ask another barrage of questions.

They kept walking. Others passed them, obviously eager to get out of the maze, too.

"You are a *gut* man, Micah Lapp," she said as Olivia's head dropped onto his shoulder. The little girl still coughed fitfully as she slept. Jayden had fallen asleep fifteen minutes earlier.

"I try to be." He gave her a cockeyed grin. "Glad to know I'm succeeding at least some of the time."

"I meant what I said. You're a *gut* man." *Too* gut *for me*, she added to herself.

Micah deserved a *wunderbaar* woman who hadn't ever treated him like dirt beneath her shoes. He should have a wife who was as devoted to a plain lifestyle as her sister, Priscilla, and who could make him a fine home.

The thought sliced through her like a blade, and she bit her lower lip to keep it from trembling. She didn't watch where she was going and stumbled over a stone, gripping Jayden more tightly so she didn't drop him.

Micah caught her arm. "What's wrong, Katie Kay? You look sick. Are you feeling bad?"

"I'm okay." She stepped away from him. For a moment, she wished he'd refused to let her go, because she'd felt safe with his wide hands curving along her arms. *Don't let your fear betray you.* "Let's keep going."

What did she want from him? He'd been worried about her and the *boppli* when he drove her to the midwife's clinic. As well, he'd taken care of her when he discovered her wandering along the road, but wouldn't he have done the same for anyone he encountered? There was no question that he was a fine man. She'd let her heart lead her to him once, and that had been disastrous. So what did she want from him *now*?

Did she want him to treat her like he used to before they walked out together? That had been such an easy time between them. He'd made her laugh and feel special without putting her on a pedestal as other guys did. Sometimes, back then, that had annoyed her because she'd liked when the young men admired her and told her how splendid she was. As Austin had until the night he'd persuaded her to drink too much. How stupid she'd been dumping Micah when he treated her with kindness and respect and honesty. And then she'd let herself be beguiled by a man who had never really cared for her.

Suddenly Katie Kay caught her breath when she saw familiar silhouettes on the other side of the stalks. The straw hats and *kapps* told her who they were.

Grabbing DJ's hand, she sprinted in the direction they'd come. She ran until she came to another dead end, paying no attention to the *kind*'s questions. She gasped for breath and fought not to cry.

When Micah came around the corner and stared at her, she blinked hard to hold in her tears. He set the abruptly wide-awake Olivia on her feet as he asked, "Why did you flee, acting as jumpy as oil on a hot griddle?"

"I saw people who looked like our neighbors." She wouldn't say the word *Amish* aloud for fear of being overheard.

His eyes widened a moment and then narrowed. "So you ran in the opposite direction without bothering to identify them?"

"I couldn't let them see me." She glanced at Olivia, who was clinging to Micah and coughing again.

"You're going to encounter someone else who knows you eventually, Katie Kay. How long are you going to try to play hide-and-seek?"

"I don't think I—"

"There's the gist of the problem. You don't think things through."

She raised her chin. "I don't need you lecturing me, Micah Stoltzfus."

"No, you need—" He halted as the little girl doubled over with her coughing. Scooping Olivia up, he held one hand out to DJ. "C'mon. What *we* need to do is find our way out of here and take Olivia home so she can get warm again. So we all can get warm. You and I can talk later, Katie Kay."

She nodded. She wanted to groan when she saw lazy snowflakes drift onto them. She'd wondered how it could get any worse in the corn maze, and now she had her answer.

As if she'd said that aloud, Micah mused, "If it keeps snowing, at least we can see other people's footprints and follow them."

She trudged after Micah, holding Jayden close and hating the sound of Olivia's coughs. Keeping her head down, she resisted peeking out from under her eyelashes to look for any plain folk.

A sweet and spicy aroma tickled her senses, and she said, "Micah, wait! Don't you smell it?" As Micah sniffed, she added, "The guy at the entrance said when we smelled pumpkin pie, we'd be close to the exit."

"*Right* close. We need to keep going right until we find the way out."

"I hope you're right... I mean, correct."

He didn't smile at her attempt to ease the tension. She hadn't expected he'd laugh out loud, but she thought his scowl might ease.

In a couple more turns, they reached the exit. Sean rushed forward to take Olivia, who was coughing hard again. As Gemma pulled out the *kind*'s inhaler, Katie Kay felt the overwhelming urge to say something, but she wasn't sure for which mistake she should apologize first.

Chapter Eleven

As the week started out, Katie Kay kept herself busy with work at the Donnellys' house. Monday and Tuesday and Wednesday mornings, she oversaw breakfast, getting DJ ready and out the door in time to get on the bus, cleaning the kitchen and doing laundry. For the first time since she'd come back to Paradise Springs, she hadn't lost her breakfast within an hour of eating it. Her stomach was queasy but didn't roil as it had since she'd become pregnant. The fear she'd have morning sickness for the full nine months eased.

Though Katie Kay's nausea had lessened, as each day passed, Gemma seemed to have a tougher time moving because she was gaining weight at a surprising speed. Her doctor had suggested she do less and rest more, a fact she hadn't mentioned.

Katie Kay knew only because Sean had explained what Gemma's obstetrician had said. "Can you keep an eye on her, Katie Kay, and suggest she stay in bed?"

"Ja." She didn't add that she intended to do more for the generous woman who had welcomed her into her home as if she were a long-lost sister. In fact, Gemma

was more accepting of Katie Kay than her real older sister had been.

She didn't need Sean's hints that she would have to be subtle or Gemma would keep working as she had… to prove she could, despite the burgeoning belly that suggested she was carrying more than one *boppli*. Tests had said otherwise, but Katie Kay knew they weren't always right.

By midmorning, Gemma had gone into the bedroom she shared with Sean to rest.

Katie Kay decided to make cookies so the *kinder* could help. That way she could keep an eye on them and they'd stay quiet. Maybe Gemma would be able to sleep.

However, Olivia, who'd had a runny nose and a hacking cough until yesterday, acted as if climbing onto a chair took too much energy. She made one attempt, slipped and began crying.

Hushing the little girl, Katie Kay assured her that she didn't have to help bake the cookies. Olivia agreed, shocking her. The little girl was usually the first one to volunteer whenever something was baked. Now, the *kind* continued to cry on and off until Jayden looked at his big sister with the same anxiety Katie Kay felt.

Katie Kay realized Olivia might be sicker than she'd been the night before. Her own younger sisters had made the same sounds that were halfway between a sob and a whine when they hadn't been feeling well. Putting her hand on the little girl's forehead, she frowned when she felt the unmistakable heat of a fever. She'd thought Olivia was getting better this morning. The *kind* hadn't coughed once during breakfast.

Picking Olivia up, Katie Kay placed her on the sofa. She set a pillow behind the little girl's head before taking a bright blue afghan off the back and spreading it over the fussy *kind*. Olivia turned her face toward the cushion and continued to sob. No, she wasn't crying, Katie Kay realized, appalled. Olivia was gasping for breath.

When two applications from Olivia's inhaler didn't help, Katie Kay looked from the little girl to the stairs. Should she disturb Gemma? If Olivia had a cold, as they'd suspected earlier in the week, keeping her *mamm* away would be wise.

But Katie Kay's mind was made up for her when Olivia coughed so hard she almost vomited. After giving the little girl a spoonful of honey to ease her sore throat, she ran up the stairs, taking two at a time.

She opened the door but didn't wait for Gemma to reply. Throwing it open, she said, "Gemma, I'm sorry to disturb you."

Pushing herself awkwardly to sit on the mussed bed, Gemma rubbed her eyes as if she were no older than her daughter. "You don't need to apologize. What's wrong?"

"It's Olivia. She's feeling worse than yesterday."

"There's another bug going around the school. DJ probably brought it home to her, and with her resistance down, she caught it. Let me check her."

"If it's contagious, maybe you should stay away from her. You don't want to get sick, too. Not at this point in your pregnancy."

"I've been exposed already."

Katie Kay nodded, realizing Gemma was right. She helped Gemma out of bed and then followed her into the living room. Locking her fingers together in front of her, Katie Kay murmured an almost-silent prayer that Olivia was already taking a turn for the better.

She knew her prayer hadn't been answered when

Gemma put her hand on the little girl's forehead and gasped. "She's burning up."

"We need to call your *doktor*. What's his name?"

Without looking up, Gemma said, "Dr. Stafford! His number is on the wall by the phone."

Rushing into the kitchen—which was splattered everywhere with the eggs, sugar and flour Jayden was continuing to stir on the table—Katie Kay grabbed the phone and punched in the number circled in red on the paper tacked to a bulletin board. The phone was answered on the second ring, and a computerized voice asked her to choose a prompt. The first choice was to push three if it were an emergency. She pressed the button.

Another voice came on the phone. This time a real woman's voice.

Katie Kay said as she hurried into the living room, "I'm calling for Gemma Donnelly. Her daughter, Olivia, is running a very high temperature. Here she is." She thrust the phone in Gemma's hand.

Going to the sink, Katie Kay dampened a clean cloth. She placed it on Olivia's head while Gemma spoke to the *doktor*'s office. The little girl was too quiet except for the rasps as she struggled to draw in another breath and let it out.

Gemma ended the call and then made another. This one to Sean, Katie Kay guessed when Gemma said the *doktor*'s office had told her to get Olivia to the closest hospital's emergency room right away.

Everything became a blur as Katie Kay packed a small bag with snacks and drinks and Olivia's favorite stuffed toy. Jayden kept asking what was wrong, and she paused long enough to open the bag of chocolate chips and tell him to pour them into the bowl. That occupied him while she bundled Olivia into her warmest coat, giving Gemma time to get her own on.

Then the Plain and Simple Solutions van squealed into the driveway. Sean rushed in. He and Gemma took Olivia and left at a speed that wasn't safe on the twisting road.

Katie Kay sent prayers after them and closed the door. She kept praying while she helped Jayden stir the cookie dough and put the first tray into the oven. When she realized she'd forgotten to turn the oven on, she pulled out the sheet and set the oven to preheat. She turned on *Sesame Street* for Jayden; then she began trying to mitigate the damage a two-year-old with a spoon and a bowl of flour could do to a kitchen when nobody was supervising him.

She was rinsing the dishcloth for the umpteenth time to get wet flour out of it when the front door opened. She wasn't surprised when she heard Micah's voice. Drying her hands on a dish towel, she hurried into the living room.

Micah was giving Jayden a hug but looked at her and asked, "What's happened? Sean got a call at the job site and left. He shouted that he'd explain later. He couldn't then because it was an emergency. The next thing I know, the van is tearing up the road. What's happened?" He glanced around the otherwise empty living room. "Is Gemma okay?"

"She's fine. Olivia's sick. We called their *doktor*, and they told Gemma to take Olivia to the hospital."

"Hospital?" His face became ashen. "What happened?"

Katie Kay shrugged. "I'm not sure. As you know, she's been coughing the last couple of days, but it stopped late yesterday, so Gemma thought she was getting better. So did I until Olivia started having trouble breathing. That's why Gemma was told to get her to the hospital as fast as possible." She wrapped her arms around herself, wishing he'd hug her as he had Jayden. "Micah, they told her not to wait for 911 to respond because they were concerned there would be too much of a delay in the EMTs arriving."

"Ach!" He dropped to sit on the nearest chair. "I didn't realize it was serious."

"Sean told you it was an emergency."

"I know, but…" He raked his fingers through his dark hair. "I guess I didn't want to believe it."

That was the truth. Micah hadn't wanted to imagine something horrible happening to the family he felt as close to as his own. Having the *doktor* tell Gemma to get Olivia to the hospital faster than the ambulance could was frightening. No wonder Sean hadn't paused to explain what was going on.

Poor little Olivia.

As Katie Kay had, he'd thought the little girl had caught a cold on Saturday. He smothered a shudder as he thought of how he, Katie Kay and the *kinder* had gotten lost in the corn maze for hours. If they'd gotten out faster, would Olivia now be playing with her little brother and asking her customary dozens of questions?

God, be with her and with her family. And with those of us who love her, so we can be strong for her and her family. Please…

"How did you get here?" Katie Kay asked, interrupting his prayer.

Her face was so pale the flour on her cheek was barely visible. Her hands shook as if she were sick, too, but she guided Jayden to the sofa and gave him his favorite picture book to read.

Standing, Micah followed her into the kitchen where she began to scrub the flour-sprinkled table with the dishcloth. "I hitched a ride with one of the men on the construction crew working on another house. He dropped me off at the crossroads, and I hoofed it here as fast as I could. What can I do to help?"

She opened her mouth to reply but halted when the phone rang.

Micah reached it in a pair of steps. Clicking it on, he said, "Hello. This is the Donnellys."

"Thank the good Lord, Micah!" came Sean's voice through the phone. The connection was clear, so Micah could hear the quaver in his friend's words. "I'm sorry I had to leave you—"

"Don't worry about it. How's Olivia?"

What Sean had to say was to the point. The *doktors* had diagnosed her with pneumonia, which was complicated by her asthma, but they wanted to run more tests. "From what we're being told, they'll be keeping her here overnight."

"Don't worry," he repeated. "Katie Kay and I will watch the boys. How are you and Gemma holding up?"

"I wish she'd be more careful, but she's refused to leave Olivia's bedside. The staff has brought in a recliner so she can put up her feet because her ankles are swelling, and that's a bad sign in a pregnant woman."

"What can I do?"

"Pray, my friend. Pray."

"I'm already doing that."

"Don't stop. We could use all the prayers we can get right now."

He hung up the phone after his friend told him that

he'd call back with any updates. Micah felt helpless, but thanked the *gut* Lord for the *doktors* and their knowledge.

By the time he'd finished telling Katie Kay what Sean had reported, the school bus was stopping in front of the house. DJ jumped out. She went to welcome the little boy home and explain his *mamm* had taken Olivia to see the *doktor*.

Amazed how she shared enough of the truth so DJ wouldn't panic, Micah watched while she listened to the boy talk about what he'd done at school. She acted as if nothing were more important than what he had to say. While she made lunch for them, Micah couldn't stop pacing. The boys ate, but he couldn't sit still.

Katie Kay halted him by stepping directly into his path. In not much more than a whisper, she said, "Go and be with your friend. Don't hurry back if you want to stay late at the hospital." She raised her voice so the boys could hear her say, "I can order pizza for supper. We'll be fine."

DJ and Jayden cheered at the idea of having pizza, and Micah knew she'd found the perfect way to distract them.

From him and his worry.

"I know you will be fine." His fingers rose before he could halt them and cupped her cheek. "I'm glad you're here, Katie Kay."

He'd expected her to pull away, but she smiled as she said, "Me, too. Sean and Gemma have done so much for me. I hope I can repay them a bit now. Go on!" She gave him a playful shove.

His arms reached out and encircled her before he had a chance to think. But as soon as he drew her to him, he couldn't think of anything but how her blue eyes glowed with astonishment. That he'd been bold, or at the instantaneous sparks arcing between them?

"Katie Kay…" Her name was the second sweetest thing he could imagine on his lips. Her actual lips would be the very sweetest.

"Go to your friends, Micah," she murmured. "They need you."

"But we need to—"

"We'll have time for everything else later." She plucked his arms off her and eased away. "Plenty of time, but you're going to regret even a minute lost when you could be with Gemma and Sean."

She was right. He knew that, but it took every ounce of his will to leave her standing there while he went to the phone and dialed the number of the *Englisch* driver his family used. After Gerry told him the van would be there in less than five minutes, he hung up.

"You never learned to drive?" Katie Kay asked.

"I did, but it's been so long I don't want to chance getting into an accident on the way to the hospital."

Did she believe him, or did she suspect the truth? He was too distraught to get behind the wheel of an unfamiliar vehicle. Either way, she nodded and went to refill DJ's glass with milk.

As promised, Gerry's van reached the house minutes later. Micah glanced back as he lifted his coat off the peg and pulled it on. With a strained smile, she motioned for him to hurry so he didn't keep Gerry waiting. She was trying to be brave, but he knew she was as heartsick as he was that Olivia had to spend the night at the hospital.

He wanted to tell her it would be okay, but he wasn't sure if it would.

Chapter Twelve

Though it was beginning to get dark, the porch light was on when Micah climbed out of the van in front of the Donnellys' house, thanked Gerry and headed up the walk past the three pumpkin figures the *kinder* had started. They didn't have any faces yet, and he wasn't sure when Sean would be able to help the boys finish them.

Micah moved as if he'd aged a hundred years in the past few hours. When he discovered the door was locked, he fumbled in his coat pocket for the ring of keys that included the one for the Donnellys' door. He hadn't expected he'd need it. He was glad he had the key because otherwise he would have had to ring the doorbell. Sean and Gemma never locked their door. In fact, nobody he knew did, but he guessed Katie Kay had picked up the habit while she lived in Lancaster.

Was she trying to keep out strangers, or did she fear someone she knew might come to the house while she was alone with the *kinder*? He wished he could meet Austin, the *boppli*'s *daed*. No, not meet him. Observe him from a distance. Micah wasn't sure if he could withhold his opinions if he came face-to-face with the man who had no intentions of honoring his obligations to her and her *boppli*.

He grimaced. Thinking about Austin made him feel lousier…if that was possible after the visit to the hospital room where little Olivia was hooked to oxygen, straining for each breath. Her face had been colorless, and her parents' had been almost as gray.

There were a half-dozen double rooms in the pediatric wing of the hospital, and most had at least one *kind* in it. Seeing sick *kinder* was discouraging, but he'd said a prayer for each as he walked along the quiet hallway. The nurses' hushed voices and the incessant beeps of medical machines had been the loudest sounds.

Opening the Donnellys' door, he winced when a hinge squeaked. The noise would have been muffled in day-to-day life with three active youngsters, but in the hush it was as loud as a cat screeching after having its tail trod on.

Katie Kay was sitting on the couch, rubbing her eyes as he walked into the living room. Her tousled hair fluttered around her face, and there was a mark on her left cheek where the button on a pillow had been pressed against it. She must have been resting. *Gut.* They couldn't forget in the midst of the emergency that she was pregnant and needed her rest, too.

Looking past her, though he wanted to let his eyes linger on her adorable mussiness, he was surprised to see the boys coloring at the kitchen table. They waved to him and went back to their crayons.

"They're being quiet," he said as he shrugged off his coat and hung it before entering the living room.

"There's a first time for everything." She tried to stifle a yawn but failed.

Should he stay overnight to help her with DJ and

Jayden? That might cause more trouble for Katie Kay.
A young unmarried woman, even one who was pregnant, should not have a bachelor in the house with her.
They wouldn't be alone, but two little boys wouldn't be
considered adequate chaperones. It wasn't as if Sean and
Gemma had a *dawdi haus* attached to their home that
would offer countenance to the circumstances.

But he couldn't leave her alone. He wasn't going to
be like her ex, who'd left her with the tough task and
gone merrily on his way.

"How is Olivia?" she asked before he could figure
out what to do.

"She's a sick little girl." He sat on the arm of the
overstuffed chair. He didn't trust himself to sit closer to
her. The yearning to hold her echoed through him with
every beat of his heart. "As Sean told me earlier, they're
pretty sure it's pneumonia, but they want to make certain there isn't something else wrong because she went
downhill so fast. Even for someone with asthma."

"Poor, sweet *kind.*" Pushing her hair behind her ears,
she asked, "Will you pray with me, Micah?"

"That's the best idea you've had in a long time."

She slid off the couch and turned to fold her hands
on the cushion as if it were a church bench. Kneeling
beside her, he bowed his head and continued the prayer
he'd been repeating over and over on the way home from
the hospital. *Heavenly Father, please bring Your heal-
ing to Olivia and let all of us who love her know the
comfort of Your presence.* Until Katie Kay put her hand
over his, he didn't realize he'd spoken his request aloud.

"I'm sorry if I intruded on your prayers."

"Don't be sorry," she whispered. "What you said
was perfect. *Danki.*"

She got to her feet as the boys argued over which

one of them got to use the red crayon next. Settling that debate, she opened the fridge. "How about I heat up some cider?"

"It's late," Micah replied.

She glanced at the clock on the wall beyond the television set. "It's only 5:30."

Micah wondered how the day could have gone so slowly. "I feel like I've lived a full week today."

"I know. Waiting slows a clock's hands to a standstill. The day my *mamm* died was one I thought would never end." She shook herself and forced a smile. "Would you like some warm cider?"

"*Ja.* Sounds like a *gut* idea."

Minutes later, she handed him a steaming cup. She put an ice cube in each plastic glass of cider before she gave them to the boys. When she picked up her own cup, he gestured toward the living room. She went in with him and sat on the rocker beside the sofa.

Neither of them spoke as the steam from the cups rose in front of their faces. He didn't need to see her expression to sense her melancholy. He understood too well, because he loved his partner's *kinder* as if they were his own and he'd seen Katie Kay grow close to the whole family.

"I'll call in the order for pizza," she said. "It'll probably be ready in about a half hour."

"I'll get it. The Pizza Palace isn't far from here."

"As long as you can be quick. I don't want the boys staying up late. Jayden's already been asking when his parents will be coming home. I'm not sure either boy believes me when I say Gemma and Sean will be here as soon as they can."

"It's the truth."

"But not the truth they want to hear." She took a sip

and then sighed. "I hope they will go to bed for me. They've done it before when Gemma's been tired, but they knew she was here."

"I can stay and help."

"Isn't Sean planning on you doing his work as well as yours tomorrow? You need to get your rest."

He laughed tersely. "I'm not going to sleep while I'm waiting to hear the news about Olivia. I might as well walk the floor here as at home, where I'll keep *Mamm* and the rest of the family awake."

"I can't argue with that." Looking into her cup, she said, "This isn't the time, but I don't know when we'll have any quiet again. I wanted to talk to you about what you said the day we went to the hardware store. You mentioned I always say *the boppli*, not *my boppli*. Remember?"

"Ja." He waited for her to continue because he wasn't sure why she'd brought up the uncomfortable subject now.

"The answer is simple. I'm afraid to love the *boppli*."

He hadn't expected her to say that. "Why?"

"Because if I love the *boppli*, what will I do if I have to give him or her up?"

"You've decided to surrender your *boppli* for adoption?" He almost choked on each word. Why hadn't she told him that she'd made the tough decision? He'd thought she trusted him enough again to discuss the future of her *kind* with him.

"No, but I've got to face the facts. Austin is the *daed*. If he wants custody of the little one, an *Englisch* judge could decide in his favor."

"But I didn't think he had a job to provide for a *kind*."

"He does. Off and on." Her mouth hardened. "Now that he can't depend on my tips and paycheck, he'll have to get a steadier job. His roommates won't let him sponge off them for very long." She blinked, and he realized she was struggling to hold back tears. "Even if it's not great, if he has any job at all, it's more than I have."

"But you're the *boppli*'s *mamm*. And Austin abandoned you on the side of a road in the dark on a rainy night."

"I don't know if a judge would take that into consideration."

"Why not? You and the *boppli* could have died if someone hadn't seen you or if you had caught a cold as Olivia has and become sick." He put his cup on the end table with such a thump the boys stopped talking in the kitchen. "I wish I could tell your Austin—"

"Not mine. Not anymore."

As if she hadn't interrupted, he kept going. "I'd like to tell him what I think of him." He shoved himself to his feet. "Face-to-face, man-to-man." He snorted a taut laugh. "Man-to-lizard, because no decent man would abandon his *boppli* as he has."

She jumped to her feet. "Don't joke about that, Micah."

He was taken aback. Was she defending the cur who'd treated her and her *kind* with such cruelty?

He realized how wrong he was when she added, "He isn't a man you can talk sense to, so please don't joke about it."

"I'm not joking. I would like to tell him what a mistake he's made."

"No, Micah! Promise me you won't do that." She grasped his arm. "Austin likes nothing better than to beat someone up. He bragged about the fights he got into." Stepping closer, she gazed with entreaty at him. "Promise me, Micah."

"Plain folk don't take pledges."

She copied his derisive snort. "Really? I've heard you tell Sean's kids you'll do something for them the next time you come over, and you do."

"Don't worry, Katie Kay. The chances of Austin and I meeting are pretty slim." Not giving her time to answer, he said, "As for tonight, Sean has an air mattress in the attic. I'll use that. I won't sleep much anyhow. Sean said I could check in on Olivia every few hours by calling his cell phone, and I'm going to do that."

"That sounds *gut*. If—"

The doorbell rang, and Micah glanced out the window. Who could it be? As far as he knew, The Pizza Palace, the village's sole pizza restaurant, didn't offer delivery. And they hadn't ordered yet.

His eyes widened when he saw a gray-topped buggy parked in front of the house. Not his. It was in the driveway. Who…?

Another vehicle was pulling into the driveway and stopping by his. When a woman stepped out of the first buggy, she was carrying a large basket and a padded container. Both were filled with food, he knew. It was the Amish answer to any crisis. *Komm* to offer assistance and prayer and bring food. No birth or funeral or wedding or church Sunday passed without women delivering food to share.

But that was among the plain folk. Why were these two women—no, make that three women because two women emerged from the second buggy—coming to the Donnellys' house with food? The Amish helped their *Englisch* neighbors in the midst of a disaster like a fire or a flood, but he hadn't expected to see his neighbors coming to his partner's door tonight.

They must have heard about Olivia being taken to

the emergency room at the hospital. He was amazed at how fast news spread among the Amish, even without phones or internet or social media, but that didn't explain why they were at the Donnellys' house.

"Katie Kay—"

"No!" She rushed into the kitchen and toward the laundry room. "I can't answer the door. If one of them sees me, they'll recognize me."

"You've been hiding long enough. You need to make up your mind one way or the other."

"I can't." Her voice broke. "Not yet. Not when these *kinder* need me."

He started to retort that she was using the boys as an excuse, but then, as he looked at her strained expression, he knew she was speaking the truth. She hadn't always since she returned from Lancaster; yet she was being honest now. Another change. Was she being changed by her time with the Donnellys and him? He'd like to think that, but he didn't want to fool himself about her again. Sean's favorite *Englisch* saying raced through his head over and over.

Fool me once, shame on you. Fool me twice, shame on me.

The doorbell rang again, and Micah knew he couldn't stand there until she saw sense. Grumbling at her stubborn inability to decide, he walked to the door. He heard the laundry room door closing as he opened the front one.

He'd recognized the caramel-colored horse pulling the buggy parked in front of the house. And he knew the woman standing on the steps, offering him a covered dish wrapped in pale blue towels.

"Do you want to come in, Cinda?" he asked.

Cinda's husband, Atlee Bender, was a minister in

the district where Micah lived. "I must get home to my family," she said, "but I heard about the sick *kind* and how you're helping. I hope your friend's boys will enjoy these noodles as much as mine do."

"Danki," he said as he took the warm casserole from her and the basket redolent with the aroma of freshly baked bread. "It's kind of you to deliver this."

"You're welcome, Micah. We will be praying for the little girl." Not giving him a chance to say more, she raised her black shawl over her bonnet of the same color and walked away into the windy evening. As she climbed into her buggy, another was pulling into the driveway.

For the next hour, Micah was kept busy answering the door as, one after another, the members of the *Leit* arrived at the house with food. Some brought one dish; others delivered food from themselves and from their extended families. DJ helped him carry the gifts into the kitchen. Even Jayden lent a hand when Micah could entrust him with something that couldn't break if dropped. The fridge was soon full, and bowls were stacked high on the kitchen table and counter. As he thanked each person for their time and the food, as well as for their prayers for Olivia's health, he didn't keep track of who had brought what. He would see the dishes were returned on a church Sunday, and each family would collect their own. No one expected praise for their generosity or the food he was certain would be delicious.

Darkness fell, and the last buggy was rolling toward Paradise Springs as Micah closed the door with his shoulder. He balanced a pie in one hand. *Snitz*, by the aroma of apples and cinnamon. In the other he held a basket covered by a miniature quilt. He guessed, though the food had been delivered by his neighbor Fannie Beiler, the pie had been made by *Mamm* and the little quilt sewn by his sister-in-law, Leah.

His eyes widened when he saw Katie Kay behind him. She held out her hands, and he handed her the food. When DJ stood on tiptoe to see into the basket, she tilted it enough so he could see the blueberry and cranberry muffins beneath the tiny quilt.

"Can I have one?" he asked.

"Me, too!" Jayden wasn't able to peek into the basket, but he wanted whatever his brother was getting.

"Supper is soon," Micah began.

"You might as well start," Katie Kay said with a warning glance at him, "by choosing one muffin each. Just one. Okay?"

The *kinder* cheered, and he knew she'd made the right decision. The little boys needed to have something to help take their minds off why their sister and their parents weren't there.

She gave him the pie as she knelt so each *kind* could select a treat from the basket. The boys pondered the decision as if the rest of their lives depended on it.

Micah remembered times when he and his twin had been presented with a similar choice. They could spend five minutes or more trying to decide between a chocolate cupcake with white frosting and a white cupcake with chocolate frosting. *Mamm* never rushed them, letting them choose on their own.

Exactly as Katie Kay was doing with Sean's boys.

When DJ and his little brother were perched on their chairs, eating their before-supper treat, Katie Kay began to sort out the food. She put dishes in the fridge, rearranging what was already in there to make room. Others she stored in the freezer. Another few she set on the counter, but she didn't have enough space, so she had to stack others on top of dishes that could support them.

Micah looked around in astonishment. "I didn't expect them to bring this."

"You didn't?" She faced him, her face bright with a smile. "You have been spending too much time among the *Englischers*. You know the *Leit* never fails to appear with food or whatever else is needed when a family has troubles."

"But they came here. To an *Englisch* house."

She laughed. "Maybe you don't get it because you weren't raised in a bishop's house, but reaching out to those in need isn't based on whether the recipient is plain or not." She took his hands in hers and looked at him. In her eyes for the first time since she'd returned from Lancaster, he saw joy and contentment. "Don't you understand? Though the Donnellys are *Englisch*, Sean is your partner. It makes him a part of your community, and the *Leit* consider them part of their community, too, because you are one of them."

"Not a part of *your* community?"

She dropped his hands. "Let's enjoy this moment for what it is, Micah. Can't you, just this once, think about now and stop worrying about the future?"

"I don't worry about the future much."

"You talk about it all the time! When we were walking out, you spoke constantly about the life you had planned for yourself. You only stopped talking about that when you began outlining the life you'd planned for us."

He stared at her, shocked. "I didn't realize. I was excited at the idea of what the future could hold."

"But if you look solely to the future, you're going to miss what's right in front of you. The life you have with your friends and your family now. You don't want to look back at this time and wish you'd treasured it more, ain't so?" She sighed. "Let me get supper for you and the boys. Why don't you go and bring down the air mattress? The boys will like watching you inflate it. Then we'll have our meal and see what the rest of the day brings, one minute at a time. Does that work for you?"

"*Ja.*"

"*Gut.*"

As she turned away, he didn't move. Again he was astonished at the realization that he was beginning to trust her enough to listen to what she had to say. Had he lost his mind? He'd asked himself that over and over, but this time he didn't have an answer.

Micah went to get the air mattress out of the attic and then checked that his horse was set for the night, while Katie Kay let the boys pick out which food they would have for supper, though she insisted they select a casserole, as well as dessert. Her own mouth watered while she watched them try to choose between the spice cake and one of the half-dozen pies arranged in a double row on the counter between the stove and the fridge.

At last the boys settled on a cold spaghetti salad made with pepperoni and green peppers. She selected rolls and warmed them in the oven. DJ helped her set the table while Jayden went to watch for Micah.

The little boys chattered about the food they were going to have. She wondered if they'd be able to sit still long enough to eat. Most of the afternoon, the boys had been like balls bouncing in every direction and never coming to a complete stop. She'd been surprised they'd colored as long as they had.

When Micah entered the kitchen, bringing cold air

with him, DJ and Jayden scrambled to get in their chairs and booster seats. She waited until Micah had taken off his coat and hat and scarf and hung them up. Once he was seated, she put a basket with the rolls in the center of the table and took her chair. The empty ones were a blatant reminder of the missing members of the family.

"Micah, why don't you say grace so we can get started?" she asked.

"*Say* grace?" He frowned, clearly questioning if she'd forgotten the Amish tradition of thanking God in silence.

"*Ja.* I think saying grace aloud tonight would be nice." She glanced at the two boys before looking at Micah again.

He nodded. "Very nice. DJ, Jayden, will you bow your heads while we thank the Lord for this *gut* food?"

Both boys complied. When Jayden reached out to take Katie Kay's hand and his brother's, hot tears filled her eyes. His short fingers trembled, and she wondered why they were trying to pretend nothing was wrong.

Micah took her other hand, and she raised her eyes to meet the worry in his. She wanted to remind him that God was with the Donnellys at the hospital, as well as with the four of them at the house, but saying that when the boys were listening might upset them more.

"*Danki*, Lord," Micah said, "for bringing us here tonight to enjoy the generosity of our neighbors. Let them know in their hearts how welcome and blessed their gifts are to this family. Watch over each of us tonight and bring us together again as soon as possible. Amen."

Katie Kay echoed, "Amen."

From the boys, she heard a smothered sniff and a half sob. She squeezed Jayden's hand and whispered, "Pass it on."

She saw DJ brighten when his little brother pressed his hand. Not giving them a chance to get lost in fear again, she scooped out servings of the cold spaghetti salad for the youngsters. Micah buttered them each a roll, and soon the kids were focused on eating.

Katie Kay did the same and found she was hungrier than she'd thought. She hadn't had more than a handful of crackers at midday. She didn't need the midwife telling her to eat wisely. She offered a silent apology to the little one inside her.

When Micah got up at the end of the meal and searched the counter, she asked what he was doing. "I thought we'd have my *mamm*'s *snitz* pie."

She stiffened. "Wanda was here? She didn't see me, did she?"

"She didn't come herself but sent a pie over in a cooler along with what her next-door neighbor and a couple of the other ladies along our road prepared." He leaned one hand on the counter as he lowered his voice so the boys wouldn't overhear. "You can't hide forever."

"Now isn't the time to discuss this." She cut her eyes toward the table where DJ and Jayden were watching them, eager for dessert.

It was easy to see the reluctance clinging to Micah as he nodded. She longed to tell him she knew that he was right. She'd known it when she went to hide in the laundry room, but the words wouldn't emerge past her lips. Her emotions were as tangled as a basket of yarn.

Jayden didn't ask about his *mamm* and *daed* until Katie Kay had tucked him in after listening to the boys say their prayers. She tried to comfort him when he began to cry. She sat on his bed and put her arms around him. At the same time, his big brother, DJ, began to sniff and his lower lip quivered.

Micah didn't hesitate. He hugged the little boy and spoke so softly Katie Kay couldn't hear what he'd said. What mattered was that DJ did, and in a few minutes he wiggled beneath the covers.

Once Jayden saw his brother was willing to sleep, he stretched out, too, and Katie Kay drew the blankets over him again. She gave each boy a kiss on the cheek and promised to wake them when their parents and sister came home. She guessed they would be up at first light, long before the hospital released Olivia.

Making sure the night-light was on in the hall and the other one in the bathroom, she drew the bedroom door almost closed. She stood outside the room for a few minutes, but neither boy rushed out. Soon it was silent inside, and she hoped they'd found comfort in sleep.

She motioned for Micah to lead the way down. *"Danki,"* she said as she reached the bottom of the stairs. "I'm not sure I would have been able to convince them to settle if you hadn't come in."

"You would have."

"Maybe." She paused with her hand on the newel post. "You're going to be a *gut daed*, Micah Stoltzfus."

"And you will be a *gut mamm*, Katie Kay Lapp."

Her fingers went to her slightly rounded abdomen. "Do you really think so?"

"Fishing for compliments?"

"I'm not looking for compliments. I'm looking for the truth." She sat on the sofa and looked at him. "I'll be truthful and say I'm not sure I'll be able to take care of this *boppli*. I left home in part because I was tired of tending to everyone else."

"I didn't realize that until you started mentioning a few things. I hope, if you go home, you'll find the situation easier to bear."

If you go home. Before this, Micah had insisted she should go home. Now he acted as if he doubted she'd make the choice.

The sudden urge to weep swept over her. There had been disappointment in his words. And why shouldn't he be disappointed in her? She was in herself.

Chapter Thirteen

If Micah had any lingering doubts about Katie Kay being a *gut mamm*, they would have vanished when she kept the boys to their normal schedule the next morning while she also got the laundry started. She didn't give them false assurances about their sister but also acted as if she believed everything would turn out for the best.

It wasn't an act, he realized, when she helped DJ put on his windbreaker and backpack. As Gemma did each day, she urged him to have a *gut* time at school and to listen to his lessons.

Suddenly DJ looked upset. When Katie Kay asked what was wrong, he motioned for her to bend toward him. He cupped his hand and began to whisper in her ear.

She hooked a finger in the kerchief she wore over her hair and drew it aside so she could hear him. When he finished, she smiled. "Don't worry. I'll take care of that, DJ."

The little boy gave her a grin and a hug that almost knocked her off her feet. As she went with DJ to the door, Jayden followed, asking for a hug of his own. She lifted him and blew a kiss in his hair. He giggled and wrapped his short arms around her neck. With the little boys, Katie Kay went out to wait for the school bus.

Curious what DJ had whispered in her ear, Micah refilled his cup with *kaffi* before going to a window with a view of the front yard. Wind blew through the few leaves remaining on the trees and tugged at the black sweater Katie Kay wore over her jeans. She put up one hand to keep her navy kerchief from flying off.

The way she dressed matched how she stood between two communities—the plain one and the one inhabited by *Englischers*. Glancing around the modern kitchen with its electric stove, refrigerator and dishwasher reminded him how he spanned those two worlds himself, though he was committed to his Amish life. But he'd miss his interactions with the Donnellys and other *Englischers* if the *Leit* decided to change the *Ordnung* and prohibit a plain man from working with a non-plain man. That wouldn't happen, but it did show him that he wasn't different from Katie Kay in many ways.

With red lights flashing, the school bus stopped by the driveway. DJ hurried to get on board.

Katie Kay set Jayden down and held his hand while they waved to his brother until the bus rumbled to a start. When she walked with Jayden to the house, she swung their hands between them.

Micah edged back so she didn't catch him watching them. One thing was clear. All of Katie Kay's thoughts were focused on the *kinder*. Where was the proud woman who had insisted on commanding everyone's attention wherever she went? She wasn't the same person she'd been a year ago. With a wry laugh, he acknowledged he wasn't the same person he'd been then either.

Katie Kay came into the kitchen accompanied by the sound of one of Jayden's favorite educational shows.

Micah couldn't restrain his curiosity longer. "What did DJ tell you?"

"He wanted to remind me that today was his turn to bring snacks."

"Snacks?"

She smiled. "Didn't your *mamm* ever send treats to school for the scholars?"

"Ja."

"Gemma told me it's the same in *Englisch* schools. The parents take turns sending in a healthy treat for snack time."

"*Mamm*'s treats were sweet rather than healthy."

She laughed. "I think DJ's classmates would prefer Amish cookies or cupcakes or pie squares, but his teacher insists on healthy snacks. The last time Gemma went shopping, she got grapes and celery and carrots for him to take in. Once they're cut up, they'll make great finger food snacks for the scholars."

"I'll drive you over to the school."

"Danki. I was going to ask how to get there. DJ's directions were pretty confusing."

Whatever Micah might have said was forgotten when the phone rang. Reaching for it, he heard Sean's exhausted voice on the other end. There was nothing new to report because Olivia's condition hadn't changed. Gemma wanted to let Katie Kay know it was DJ's turn to bring snacks.

"All taken care of," Micah reassured his friend.

Relieved, Sean said he'd call later in the day to give them an update. When Micah told his partner he planned to stop by the hospital again that afternoon, he heard gratitude in Sean's voice.

"You are a *gut* friend," Katie Kay said when he hung up the phone. "Sean and Gemma are blessed to have you." She opened the fridge door before he could reply he wasn't the only one they were depending on, but he wasn't sure how Katie Kay would take his words. The girl who had coveted compliments was a woman who seemed embarrassed by them.

Within the hour, Katie Kay had the fruit and vegetables prepared. She helped Jayden with his coat while Micah hitched Rascal to the buggy.

The little boy squirmed on the seat, excited about riding in the buggy to his big brother's school. He let out a cheer when the low, red brick building came into view. Katie Kay warned him to be quiet when they went inside, and he pretended to zip his lips closed. Micah wondered how long the *kind* would remember his promise.

Checking in at the office, they were directed to a room a couple of doors down the hall. Micah opened the door, and every student in the room turned to stare at the door. DJ ran to them. Taking them by the hand, he tugged them into the room.

He turned and announced, "This is my daddy's friend Micah and his friend Katie Kay."

Micah hid his chuckle when he saw Katie Kay's cheeks flush a pretty pink as speculation bloomed in the teacher's eyes. She should recall if a kindergarten teacher took everything a *kind* said as the truth, then the teacher was going to have to swallow a lot of tall tales.

"This is the first time we've ever had our morning snacks delivered in a buggy," said the teacher as she came to collect the trays covered with aluminum foil. "Thank you for bringing them. Will you be picking DJ up? I know his parents have given you approval to do so."

"No," he said. "He should come home on the bus."

"All right." She hesitated and then said, "DJ told us his little sister is ill."

"*Ja*, she is," Katie Kay replied. "That's why we brought the snacks instead of Gemma. We'll let her know you were asking about Olivia."

"Thank you." The teacher opened her mouth, then closed it and gave them a smile before turning to her students. "Let's tell DJ's brother and his friends thank you for bringing us snacks."

"Thank you," said the scholars as one.

Jayden was reluctant to leave. His gaze focused on an easel with paints beside it. Micah herded the little boy ahead of him out of the room. As soon as they emerged into the crisp day, Jayden began chattering like a blue jay about everything he'd seen and asking when he could go with DJ to school.

Katie Kay answered each question until the *kind* became fascinated with watching cars and trucks pass the buggy. He jerked his arm up and down, and he grinned when one of the tractor-trailers blew its horn. Fortunately Rascal wasn't bothered by the noise.

"DJ's teacher seems nice," Micah said as he turned them off the main road. He didn't have to watch for the big trucks so he glanced at Katie Kay. "But I could tell she wanted to ask us a bunch more questions."

"*Englischers* are curious about plain folk." She smiled. "Otherwise, there wouldn't be so many of them spending their vacations in Lancaster County. You must get plenty of questions from your clients."

"Not really." He rested his elbows on his knees and held the reins loosely. "Most of them, whether they're Amish or *Englisch*, are interested in getting the work finished. That's what I get questions about. Is it okay if I drop you off at the house and then head over to the hospital?"

"Of course." Her smile warmed. "I don't think I could stop you from being with your friend."

He looked away. She wasn't right. He could think of a reason to remain with Katie Kay, but he'd be a fool to kiss her again and risk his heart once more.

Fool me once, shame on you. Fool me twice, shame on me.

When, the following day, Micah said he wasn't going to work again, Katie Kay was relieved. Throughout the night while she tried to get the boys to go to sleep, she worried about Micah being on a roof when his thoughts were elsewhere. A single wrong step, and he could have been heading to the emergency room, too.

Only an hour before dawn, Micah had convinced the little boys to sleep on the air mattress with him. She doubted he got any sleep, because his eyes were shadowed with deep gray arcs. She'd snatched less than an hour herself before getting up to make breakfast.

As they were finishing the meal, sharing more of the freshly made bread delivered to the house, Micah asked the boys if they wanted to help him clean out the van after he pulled it into the garage. She was pleased that he realized the wind was too strong and cold for the little boys to spend much time outside. Nobody spoke of DJ going to school because the *kinder* were dragging with exhaustion.

She waited until the little boys had followed Micah outside and then she found the phone number of the school. The woman who answered said that if DJ stayed home more than a couple of days, they would make arrangements to get his lessons to him.

"Tell Gemma and her husband that we're praying for them and their little girl," the woman said before hanging up.

Katie Kay's fingers lingered on the phone as she set it in its cradle. Those simple words offered such comfort, and she'd make sure she passed them on to Gemma and Sean. Katie Kay hadn't caught the name of the woman on the phone, but she guessed Gemma would know.

Hoping that working with Micah would calm the boys enough so they'd take a nap later, Katie Kay did the breakfast dishes and cleaned the house. She was surprised how much she enjoyed taking care of a home when she wasn't being criticized for missing a cobweb or leaving dust on a table. For the first time, she began to imagine what it would be like to have a house and family of her own like Gemma did.

And a husband, too, to complete the happy picture?

A sigh drifted from her as she stopped the vacuum and began to reel up the cord. Who would want to marry her when she carried another man's *kind*?

Micah had offered, and she'd turned him down. He'd told her he wouldn't ask her again.

What a mess she'd made of her life! All her hopes of experiencing things she couldn't while among the *Leit* taunted her. She'd gotten her wish but in ways she'd never reckoned.

Katie Kay flinched when the doorbell sounded through the house. Who could it be? She glanced out a nearby window and didn't see a buggy. Inching closer to another window with a view of the porch, she gasped when she saw the tall redhead reaching to push the doorbell again.

Rushing to the door, she threw it open. "Cherokee!

Come in. What are you doing here? Why didn't you call to let me know you were coming?"

"Because I don't have a phone number for you." Cherokee wrapped her in a warm embrace.

Curvy was the best description of Cherokee Smith, who dated Austin's best friend Vinnie. Though Cherokee had never said, Katie Kay suspected she came from a wealthy family. The redhead never seemed to wear an outfit more than once, and her clothing was in the latest style from the fashion magazines she'd shared with Katie Kay while the men were watching sports or sitting on the stoop to smoke.

Today she'd draped gold bangles around her wrists, as well as a trio of necklaces over her black turtleneck sweater. Her earrings were large and gaudy with bright gems that might be costume or real. Katie Kay had no idea.

"How did you find me?" Katie Kay asked.

"Vinnie saw the license plate on the van you were driving." Cherokee winked as she added, "I had a friend do a little digging, and he found this address."

Katie Kay suspected Cherokee's friend wasn't involved with any type of law enforcement, but decided she didn't want to know why he had access to such information. She motioned toward the living room. Her friend began talking as fast and nonstop as Jayden had in the buggy yesterday. Unlike the little boy who'd been positive about the idea of going to school like his big brother, Cherokee listed every reason she had to be miserable.

Sitting on the sofa after she'd moved aside the afghan as if it were a soiled diaper, Cherokee said, "The biggest problem is you aren't around to keep Austin under control."

"I never was able to do that."

"Maybe you didn't think so, but he acted less immature when you were around. Until he found out you were…" Her gaze focused on Katie Kay's abdomen. Looking away, she added, "Then he became more of a jerk than ever."

"I'm sorry."

"*You* don't have anything to be sorry for. I wish Vinnie would spend less time with him and more time with *my* friends. He says they don't want to talk about anything interesting, and they don't like him because he drinks too much and yaks about sports all the time."

Katie Kay tried to relate to such problems, but it was impossible. She hadn't realized how far behind she'd left her life in Lancaster and the group of young adults who could hardly be called friends. They quarreled and made fun of others when they weren't around. She'd felt uncomfortable but hadn't defended anyone. Shame flooded her while Cherokee continued to complain about people Katie Kay knew and some she didn't.

When Cherokee halted in the middle of a word, her mouth dropping open, Katie Kay started to ask what was wrong. The eager voices of DJ and Jayden burst into the room as the boys ran to where she sat on the rocker. They talked at the same time, each trying to be heard, about Micah letting them help him sort out the nuts and washers stored in the van.

But the boys weren't who had caught Cherokee's attention. Behind them, Micah leaned one shoulder against the doorway. His gaze was focused on his partner's sons, and Katie Kay couldn't mistake the expression in his deep blue eyes. He wanted little ones of his own, *kinder* he could teach as he was Sean's boys.

"Who's that?" Cherokee asked, and Micah pushed away from the wall, his easy pose vanishing.

Katie Kay stood. "Micah, we have company. *Komm* and let me introduce you."

Micah walked toward her. She ignored the questions visible on his face because she couldn't answer them while Cherokee and the boys were listening.

"This is my friend Cherokee," she said, hoping her voice didn't shake. "Cherokee Smith."

If Micah was as shocked by the woman's name as Katie Kay had been the first time she'd heard it, nothing showed in his smile. "Nice to meet you, Cherokee."

"Nice to meet *you*." Cherokee eyed him with candid admiration before giving him a slow, appreciative smile.

Katie Kay curled her fingers so tightly her fingernails cut into her palms. She almost gasped at the strength of her irritation at how Cherokee was flirting with him. Cherokee had a boyfriend. She didn't need to intrude on…

Intrude on what? her rational mind demanded. It wasn't as if she and Micah were a couple. Still, she couldn't halt the jealousy searing her veins like liquid flame.

And the guilt. When she'd flirted with guys, had Katie Kay irritated other women as Cherokee was her? She'd never considered how other girls felt. Probably because she knew her flirting didn't mean anything.

Maybe Cherokee's didn't either. Thinking that failed to ease the fire of jealousy within her. She had no idea how to douse it, and it made her uneasy. Only someone in love could be jealous, ain't so? And she wasn't in love.

She gulped as she glanced at Micah, and their gazes

collided. The heat in his eyes urged her to melt right into his arms.

No! No! She couldn't be in love with him. She'd told him *twice* she didn't want to be involved with him. *Twice*! And now...

But she couldn't ignore how quivers raced through her each time his hand brushed against her, even just in passing. And his eyes, which could alter from storm-blue to the crystalline of a summer sky, invited her to find out if her memory of his kiss was as *wunderbaar* as she remembered.

She was grateful when Cherokee spoke again, freeing Katie Kay from her thoughts.

"Are these your little boys, Micah?" Her friend's grin broadened.

"No," he said. "Their parents are at the hospital with their sister, who has pneumonia."

Cherokee instantly grew serious. "Oh, I'm sorry. Is she going to be okay?"

"Ja," Katie Kay said, aware of the little boys listening to every word.

Micah excused himself and the *kinder*, so he could put an end to the conversation. She was glad when they returned to the kitchen to grab pie squares before heading to the garage.

Cherokee walked to a window. She whistled. "I understand why you didn't bother to come back, Katie Kay. Don't tell Vinnie I said this, but you've traded up. Your buddy Micah is swinging a heavy tool belt into the van as if it doesn't weigh anything. Nice muscles on that farm boy."

Katie Kay sat on the rocker, hoping Cherokee would take the hint to return to her chair. As her friend sat across from her again, Katie Kay asked, "Why did you drive here by yourself? I've heard you say too many times to count the countryside gives you hives."

"Why am I here?" Cherokee's eyes widened. "I thought it was obvious."

"It probably is to someone who's had more than three hours sleep total for the past two nights. Micah's keeping the boys busy in the hope they'll sleep tonight and not wake up every few minutes calling for their parents."

"Poor little kids." Clasping her hands on the knees of her stylish jeans, she smiled as her bangles clattered together. "I came out here to see how you're doing. Austin treated you really, really bad. I couldn't believe it when I heard what he did to you. I didn't think he would be low enough to abandon you in the middle of nowhere."

"It actually wasn't far from my family's house."

She waved aside Katie Kay's words. "That doesn't make any difference. Austin was a jerk. Vinnie thinks so, too."

"Vinnie was with us that night."

"I know." Her mouth tightened into a straight line. "I didn't talk to him for two days after I heard, but then I realized he was scared Austin would do something to him, too. If he gets kicked out of the apartment, he doesn't have anywhere else to go except to his parents' house and they won't let him come back."

Katie Kay lowered her eyes. What if she returned home and *Daed* and her sisters and brother turned her away as Vinnie's parents had him?

"Tell Vinnie not to bother arguing with Austin," she said to her friend, so she could ignore her own thoughts. "He'd be wasting his breath. I'm done with Austin."

"I'm glad you finally wised up."

"Wised up? I thought you liked Austin."

"I *love* Vinnie, and, unfortunately, Austin comes along as part of the package." Her mouth twisted. "If I could think of a reason Vinnie would listen to, I'd convince him to dump Austin. Austin is a spoiled brat who thinks only of himself. A real user and a loser, but I don't have to tell *you* that."

Had Katie Kay been any better when she'd fled Paradise Springs and gone in search of everything she thought she was missing out on? She'd heard opposites attract, but she and Austin had been too much alike.

Had been.

She dared to believe that while he lived in his extended childhood, doing as he wished and wheedling others to do what he didn't want to do, she'd grown up. Six months ago, she wouldn't have been willing to take care of someone else's *kinder*. She wouldn't have felt satisfaction in putting a *gut* meal on the table or cleaning up after the family.

"So…" Cherokee leaned forward. "Are you and cute Amish guy an item?"

She hoped that explaining how Micah had found her walking along the road in the rain would satisfy her friend's curiosity about him. But Cherokee kept asking questions. How long had Katie Kay known him? How had he gotten those great muscles? Had he asked Katie Kay out?

Katie Kay should have expected it, because her friend was obsessed with everyone's relationships, including movie stars she'd never met. Any attempts to change the subject were fruitless until Katie Kay happened to mention the plans her *daed* and Wanda Stoltzfus had made.

"Your father is getting married to Mr. Cutie-Pie Amish Guy's mother?" Cherokee sighed. "Does that

mean he's off-limits to you? That would be a shame."
Her grin returned. "You could grab him right now and
find a justice of the peace and get married."

"I'm not getting married now."

Her eyes widened. "Oh? Because of the baby? Vinnie told me that Austin said you two agreed you were
going to give it up for adoption."

"I haven't decided yet." The words tasted like sawdust in her mouth, and her stomach twisted at the idea
of abandoning her *boppli*.

"You're going to need to. After all, the kid has got
to be a complication when you're in love with a man
who's not the baby's father."

"Who said anything about love?" she snapped and
then wished she hadn't.

Cherokee chuckled. "Nobody, but I'm not stupid,
girl! You never looked at Austin—not once—like you
look at Mr. Cutie-Pie Amish Guy."

"His name is Micah!"

"I know, and you're quick to jump to his defense.
That's proof you're in love with him."

Katie Kay hadn't ever realized Cherokee was so
perceptive. Usually she hung on to every word Vinnie
spoke and didn't seem to have a single thought in her
head. There were depths to the young woman that Katie
Kay hadn't guessed existed.

"Is your dad having a big wedding? He's some
honcho, isn't he?" Not giving her a chance to answer,
Cherokee smiled and added, "Maybe you'll catch the
bouquet and your Cutie-Pie Amish Guy will take the
hint and propose."

"We don't throw a bouquet at an Amish wedding.
There isn't a bouquet, though sometimes there are flow-
ers on the tables during the wedding meal. More often,

there are vases filled with celery." She smiled. "That's one of our most cherished wedding traditions."

When Cherokee asked about other traditions, Katie Kay was relieved. They talked a half hour longer before her friend had to leave so she could return to Lancaster at the time she'd told Vinnie.

"He gets worried if I'm late," the redhead added. "Isn't that sweet?"

Katie Kay made a sound Cherokee must have taken as an affirmative because her friend stood, gave Katie Kay a hug and went to the door. With a wave of her fingertips, she was gone.

Silence fell on the living room. Cherokee may not have intended them to, but her words reminded Katie Kay that *Daed* was getting married, and he would have a much bigger family to worry about. She didn't need to cause him extra distress. It was time for her to face her mistakes.

Long past time.

But how? She bowed her head and began to pray, hoping God would listen to her heart, which was confused about everything in her life. About going home. About having the *boppli* on her own. And about what she was going to do, because Cherokee was right. She was falling in love with Micah.

Chapter Fourteen

Micah grabbed DJ and Jayden by the hands as Gemma's familiar van turned into the driveway later that afternoon. The boys yelled in their excitement at seeing their parents after two long nights apart, but Micah didn't release them until the van had stopped and the doors opened.

He smiled as Sean stepped between the boys and their *mamm* so they didn't hurt Gemma or the *boppli* in their enthusiasm. Hugging them both, Sean listened as they tried to tell him everything at once.

"We'll talk inside," Sean said, ruffling their hair. "Go with Mommy while I get Olivia."

Stepping forward to help, Micah waited until Sean lifted a swaddled Olivia out of her car seat. Micah shut the van's doors as the family surged as one toward the house. His hope to catch a glimpse of Olivia's face to see how she'd improved was foiled by the blanket.

The front door opened. Katie Kay's face was as bright with elation as the autumnal sunshine. She ushered everyone inside and then moved out of the way to let Sean carry Olivia to the couch.

The little girl looked weak, and she rasped as she

breathed, but she gave a weak smile at her brothers and Katie Kay and Micah.

While Sean set her down as if she were made of flower petals ready to blow away at the slightest breeze, Katie Kay assisted Gemma with her coat and getting to a comfortable chair. Katie Kay picked up another afghan as Sean covered Olivia with the one on the sofa. Draping the afghan over Gemma, she tucked it around her from waist to toes.

Feeling useless, Micah went into the kitchen and made *kaffi*. He brought two cups in and gave them to Sean and Gemma.

"Hope it tastes okay," he said with a weary smile.

"You made this?" asked his partner, not trying to hide his astonishment.

"Ja."

"Things have changed a lot since we've been gone, honey." Sean winked at his wife. "Who would have guessed we'd ever see an Amish man working in the kitchen? Katie Kay, how did you convince him to do that?"

Micah became uneasy when Katie Kay didn't answer.

To fill the silence that seemed oppressive to him, he said, "She made it clear if I wanted *kaffi*, I could make it myself while she was getting DJ off to school."

"I'm going to have to try that with Sean." Gemma laughed, but fatigue tainted the sound.

Katie Kay smiled but didn't speak while she watched the little boys go back and forth between their sister and their parents, happy to have them home again. When Sean put out his arms to keep Jayden from patting Olivia's cheek for the third time, Katie Kay wrapped her arms around herself and bit her lower lip.

What was she thinking? She'd been happy when Gemma and Sean had arrived with Olivia. Now Micah sensed a barrier like the one she'd thrown up the night she'd decided not to walk out with him any longer. That night, he'd been hurt and angry at how she shut herself off from him.

She was doing it again, and he had no idea why. This time would be different. He was going to find out the truth.

Just not today. He'd have to be patient, he told himself as he listened to the happily reunited family and thanked God that Olivia was alive and home.

As he sent up that prayer, he glanced toward Katie Kay. She was gone. After everything she'd done to help this family, why wasn't she celebrating with them?

Another question he didn't have an answer to. But Micah's plan got turned inside out, because just before dark, Katie Kay walked into the garage, where he was touching up the paint around the dent on Gemma's van. He rested the paintbrush on top of the open can and stood.

Without a greeting, she said, "Micah, I believe it's time."

Time? For the *boppli*? How could that be? Her stomach was so barely rounded that anyone who didn't know she was pregnant wouldn't suspect it. It couldn't be time for the *boppli* to be born.

"What?" He couldn't manage more than a single word as he wondered if he needed to call 911. Swallowing hard, he tried again. "The *boppli*—"

"It's not time for that." Her smile appeared and fled so quickly that it might have been his imagination. "It's time for me to go home."

"Home?" He sounded like he was half-asleep, repeating her words without understanding what they meant.

"*Ja.* I want to go home to my family."

He wasn't certain if she or he was more shocked when he asked, "Are you sure?"

"You've been insisting I need to reconcile with *Daed* and the rest of my family. Why are you hesitating?"

"Because I want you to be sure you're ready for what may happen."

"I'm not. I can't be, but it's time. I saw the expressions on Sean's and Gemma's faces when they came home to their boys, and I knew how much they'd hated being apart from their *kinder*. How painful it was for them!" Her voice lowered almost to a whisper. "And how painful it was for DJ and Jayden to be without them." She shook herself and squared her shoulders. "I've put my family through enough. I figured I'd go over there tomorrow and let them know I'm nearby."

"You don't plan to return home for *gut*?"

"I don't know." A faint smile eased her taut lips. "You asked me to make a decision, and so far all I've decided is I need to tell them where I am. I haven't thought beyond that."

"Why?" He'd thought the toughest choice would be deciding to go home, not whether she'd stay or not.

"The problems I left behind are still there."

He was delving into what wasn't his business. Or was it? Her family was soon to be attached to his. "Problems?"

"Mainly one. The fact I'll never meet the standards set by Priscilla, something she reminds me every time we've talked since my *mamm* died."

"Priscilla? Is she the reason you left?"

"One of them. I got tired of her lambasting me about everything I did or didn't do."

Taking her by the shoulders, he looked into her sorrowful eyes. "Do you think you're the only one who's been the target of your sister's judgmental comments?"

Her head jerked up, the sadness replaced by amazement. "You, too?"

"*Ja*, and half the people our age in the district. She's careful to say nothing when Reuben's around, but she acts as if she's the sole authority on how everything should be done."

"I didn't realize that." Tears glistened on her lashes. "I thought I was the only one—"

"Trust me. You're not." He laughed. "Remember that when we go to Reuben's house."

"You're going with me?"

He brushed her soft golden hair from her face and framed her cheeks with his hands as he leaned toward her. "I wouldn't miss it for the world, Katie Kay. I always enjoyed taking you home."

Her lips parted to speak, but he silenced her with his mouth on hers. Maybe it was the right time to kiss her. Maybe it wasn't. Either way, he wasn't going to allow the moment to escape him again.

He thought she'd push him away, but she softened against him, and everything disappeared but her fingers sliding up his arms to encircle his shoulders. Time eclipsed to the last time he'd kissed her; yet it was as if he held her for the very first time as happiness enveloped him. She fit perfectly in his arms, as if she'd been made just for him.

She drew herself back, letting her fingers glide down to entwine with his. They stood face-to-face for a moment, and then she stood on tiptoe and kissed him on the cheek.

"I always enjoyed you taking me home, Micah," she whispered.

"Then—?"

She gave him no time to ask the obvious question: Why had she stopped walking out with him if she felt that way? She slipped her hands out of his and hurried out of the garage, leaving him more confused than ever.

Micah said nothing as Katie Kay worked hard to take care of the Donnelly family the next day. She'd spent the early part of the morning getting DJ off to school and making sure breakfast was ready for the rest of the family. Both Sean and Gemma stayed close to their daughter, checking her constantly until she got cranky at their smothering attention. At that point, Katie Kay insisted that they eat a sturdy breakfast before they sickened, too. She'd guessed, quite rightly, that neither Sean nor Gemma had eaten much at the hospital. Both of them looked almost as wan as their daughter.

While the hours unfurled and she prepared the midday meal and served it, Micah wondered if Katie Kay was using Olivia's homecoming as an excuse to defer her own. He hid his surprise—and his relief—when Katie Kay asked, late in the afternoon, if he'd be ready to leave in a half hour. When he assured her that Rascal and the buggy would be set whenever she wanted to go, she went upstairs.

He wasn't sure what she was doing until she came back down. He heard smothered gasps from the Donnellys and swallowed his own. Katie Kay was dressed in plain clothing.

Sean's and Gemma's surprise was because they'd

never seen her wearing an Amish cape dress, but Micah
had forgotten how pretty she was when she dressed
plain. Her blond hair was in a miniature bun held in
place by a handful of bobby pins beneath her *kapp*,
and her cheeks were almost the same color as the warm
pink dress she wore with a black apron that concealed
her baby bump. Beneath the white *kapp*, her blue eyes
seemed brighter. Instead of the jeans she'd worn since
her return, her legs were covered in modest black socks,
and she wore scuffed, black sneakers.

He said nothing as she thanked Sean and Gemma
for welcoming her into their home. Both of them gave
her a hug and wished her well before the *kinder* embraced her, as well.

Nodding his own thanks to his friends, he held the
door for Katie Kay and followed her to the buggy. She
climbed in without his help and remained silent while
he got in, picked up the reins and gave Rascal the com-
mand to go.

The horse was eager to return to his warm stall, so he
trotted along the road leading toward Paradise Springs.
The Saturday traffic was light on the back roads, and
Micah kept to them instead of risking the rush of cars
and trucks on Route 30.

Almost ten minutes after the Donnellys' house had
disappeared past a curve in the road, Katie Kay spoke
for the first time. "*Danki*, Micah, for driving me."

"It's the least I could do, seeing as I didn't take you
home a few weeks ago."

She glanced at him and away as the buggy wheels
crunched leaves that had fallen from the trees by the
fences. Smoothing her apron over her dress, she reached
up to touch her *kapp*. "I shouldn't have cut my hair,
but..."

When her voice faded, he looked at her. She appeared so nervous that, if he hadn't known the truth, he would have guessed she was going somewhere she'd never been before. His fingers settled on her hand to calm her.

"Reuben is going to be pleased to see you. He won't care you cut your hair."

"I hope you're right."

"I *know* I'm right, and so do you. Your *daed* lives the life he preaches."

"I know that, too." Her voice sounded dull, and he took his gaze from the road to check her again.

The last of the color had drained from her face, and she sat as tense and unsure as the night he'd discovered her walking along the road. Had something he said caused this change?

"What is it?" he asked, not willing to let her hide behind the wall she'd raised between them again.

"*Daed* does live the life he preaches. I've never been able to. It's another of the reasons I had to leave, Micah. I couldn't be the bishop's perfect daughter. I'm not quiet and proper and a role model for other daughters in my *daed*'s districts. In fact, I'm the opposite. Where I go, instead of peace, there's chaos."

"You're right about that." He didn't let his smile fall away when she glared at him. Resting his elbows on his knees as Rascal continued along the familiar road, he glanced at her again. Longer this time. "Katie Kay, I've heard you talk many times about your little sister Sarann."

"She was the light of our family."

"But she was also a challenge for your family."

She frowned. "You know we didn't think of her that way. She was a blessing from God."

"Aren't you the same?"

"I'm not handicapped."

"No, you're not. At least not outwardly, but, like Sarann, you've been a challenge for your family. Do you think they love you any less than they loved Sarann?"

"Ja."

His shock at her answer must have been visible because she seemed to shrink into herself. Was this how she saw herself? Unloved by her own family? How could she think that when her *daed* had spoken well of her and was distraught when she left home?

Another bolt of astonishment struck him. Maybe she didn't know how Reuben loved each of his *kinder*. The bishop spoke of them often, admitting he couldn't hide his pride in his four living daughters and his son who helped him on the farm. Had Reuben told her that? Even if he hadn't, how could she miss how much her *daed* adored her and the rest of his family?

Realization struck him. She knew Reuben loved her siblings. She couldn't bring herself to believe he felt the same about the family's wandering lamb.

"Katie Kay Lapp," he said, "Reuben doesn't love you less than any of your siblings."

"I never said *Daed* doesn't love us."

"Then who?"

"Micah, it's not something I should be talking about beyond my family."

"But we'll soon be family. When *Mamm* marries your *daed*."

"Maybe, but we aren't family yet, and I've already said too much."

He had to accept her gentle chiding. It was true he was poking his nose where it didn't belong. He wondered if *Mamm* knew of this underlying cause for Katie Kay jumping the fence. Was it more than her older sister's pressure for her to be perfect? Curiosity about what had happened to sour Katie Kay on her family teased him, but he refused to ask. She was right. It was none of his business.

But that wouldn't stop him from trying to persuade her to tell him the truth.

Katie Kay was sure she'd forgotten how to breathe as Micah's buggy turned toward her *daed*'s house.

Toward home.

Her youngest sister, Marnita, was bringing in the laundry from the line that ran from the house to the main barn, and in the distance her brother, Lester, drove a team of five mules through a field. As the buggy drew to a stop by the white house, she saw Ina Sue, her other younger sister, walk past the kitchen window.

Where was *Daed*?

As if she'd shouted, *Daed* came striding from the barn. His bibbed denim overalls and knee-high rubber boots were covered with bits of hay and sawdust, a sign he'd been fixing something. He called a greeting to Micah, and she knew he'd recognized the buggy by the horse pulling it.

Micah took her hand and squeezed it, but he said nothing.

Katie Kay pushed open the door on her side. She climbed out and walked toward where her *daed* had stopped.

"*Daed*, it's…" Every word she'd practiced over and over fell out of her head as her *daed* stared as if he couldn't believe his eyes.

He looked old. Older than she remembered, as if she'd been gone for years instead of months. The lines in his face were gouged a bit deeper and his shoulders bent more. Was that a tremor she saw in his hands? The hands that had held the family's large Bible and had cradled a newborn as gently as a spring zephyr.

"Daed," she began again, trying to remember what she wanted to say first.

He strode forward and swept her into his arms and held her. She drew in the scents that had been a daily part of her life until the past few months. The smells of fresh air, hard work and the laundry soap the Lapps had used for as long as she could remember.

She clung to him, her eyes closed. If she opened them or moved a single muscle, the wonder of the reunion might disappear like the dreams she'd had of this moment. In the distance, she heard Marnita yelling for Ina Sue to come out of the house. Pounding feet rushed toward them and other arms were flung around her. She savored the embrace of the family she'd thought might be lost forever.

Daed stepped back but kept his eyes on her as the wrinkled planes of his face eased into a smile. Tears ran along his cheeks, falling into his beard. Marnita used her apron to wipe away her own, and Ina Sue leaned against her younger sister before whirling to pull Lester into the family circle as he came running to learn why they were shouting.

"Katie Kay…" *Daed* whispered her name as if it were a prayer.

She realized it was, because he was thanking God for bringing her home. *"Daed*, I'm sorry. Please forgive me."

"There is no need to ask for forgiveness, my dear daughter. As Jesus told us in His parable of the man with two sons, when the prodigal son returned home, the whole family celebrated because the one who had been lost was found." He embraced her again. "Now *you* have found your way home, and you're here with your family, where you belong."

Her siblings joined into the group hug. She squeezed them, not wanting to let go of this moment or them.

"*Danki*, son," she heard *Daed* say and realized he was talking to Micah.

Katie Kay's sisters led her toward the house as Lester went to unharness the team and join them. Both of her sisters talked at the same time, reminding her of DJ and Jayden. As they stepped onto the porch, she glanced over her shoulder.

Happiness, greater than when she'd been in her *daed*'s arms, swept over her when she saw *Daed* with his arm draped over Micah's shoulders as they followed. Both of them were grinning like cats with a fresh bowl of milk.

She hated ruining their *gut* cheer, but she paused and turned to face them. She waited until they reached where she stood with her puzzled sisters. Watching her *daed*'s face, she whispered, "I'm pregnant, *Daed*."

"Your *boppli* is as welcome as you are here," he said as if she'd announced she was making his favorite pie for supper.

Tears burst out of her as his words touched the part of her heart that had ached every hour she'd been gone. When he hugged her again, she heard the house door open and close. She saw her siblings had gone inside.

Micah started to do the same, but *Daed* put up his hand to halt him.

Realizing what *Daed* wanted to know, she said, "The *boppli* isn't Micah's." She pushed the rest of the truth out. "The *boppli*'s *daed* is *Englisch*."

"And where is he?" His voice was calm, but she heard the thunder of anger resonating beneath his words.

"Out of our lives, *Daed.*"

He took a deep breath and let it out in a long, slow sigh. "Is this your decision, Katie Kay?"

Was it? Austin had thrown her out of his car and his life once he knew she was going to have a *boppli. "Ja, Daed,"* she replied, knowing it was the truth. "I made a mistake, but that doesn't mean the *boppli* needs to suffer its whole life for it."

"No *boppli* is a mistake." He cupped her chin and tilted her face so she met his eyes. "Each one is God's gift to us and the future."

"*Danki, Daed.* I needed to hear that."

He glanced again at Micah. "I'm sure I'm not the first one to tell you that."

"You're not," she whispered.

Without another word, *Daed* went into the house, leaving her alone with Micah.

Katie Kay wasn't prepared for the rush of shyness flooding her. She'd never been timid with Micah, but she was now.

He must have sensed that because he said, "I'm glad everything went well."

"You knew it would."

He grinned. "If I say *ja,* you'll think I'm saying 'I told you so.'"

"You have every right to."

"No, I don't." He became serious again. "I'd prayed for a *gut* homecoming for you, but only God knows for certain what's to come. We can only hope and pray."

"You are a *gut* man, Micah Lapp," she said as she had before. "And I'm glad you are my friend."

"Is that all we are? Friends?"

Through the early twilight, she felt the intensity in his eyes. She wished she could unsay her unconsidered words. What must he think of her calling him a friend when she'd kissed him so eagerly yesterday?

Before she could say anything, he walked to his buggy, climbed in and drove away.

She stood and watched as the buggy faded into the darkness, knowing she had hurt him worse today than she ever had in the past.

Chapter Fifteen

The bench wagon was parked in the yard when Sean dropped Micah off at the Stoltzfus farm the following Monday. Thanking his partner, Micah got out and waved as the van turned around before driving toward the road. The wagon must have arrived earlier. With most Amish weddings celebrated from late October until the end of the year, the bench wagon would be making many stops in addition to the homes where church Sunday services were scheduled to be held.

Inside it were the benches for the service, as well as extra dishes and flatware for feeding the *Leit* after worshipping. That wouldn't be enough for the large number of guests *Mamm* and Reuben had invited. He suspected most people would be at the house bright and early on the wedding day to enjoy their bishop's wedding.

But he could think of only one person who'd be attending.

Katie Kay.

He knew he shouldn't have stomped off when she called him her friend, but he felt as if he was reliving the past. As before, she'd kissed him and then she'd told him she didn't consider him more than a friend. Well, it wasn't quite the same as before. Last time, she hadn't even wanted to remain friends.

He might be a coward, but he wasn't going to put his barely patched heart on the line and let her squash it like a bug.

Sean had been curious about what had happened, and Micah had told him how Reuben had welcomed his wayward daughter home. Nothing else. His partner had given him odd looks. Sean knew there was more to the story but respected him enough not to ask. Gemma was as circumspect.

Another barrier between him and the people who were important to him, and he hated it.

As he approached the wagon, he saw two of his brothers there. His twin, Daniel, and their older brother Jeremiah, the only Stoltzfus sibling besides Micah who didn't have a spouse or plans in the next few weeks to marry. Micah called a greeting, though he would have gladly walked past and sought the sanctuary of the room he soon wouldn't share with Daniel after a lifetime together.

"We figured helping Ezra get ready for the wedding was the least we could do," Jeremiah said with a smile.

Daniel added, "Which is why we're doing it."

Laughing along with his brothers and surprised he could pretend to be happy enough to laugh, Micah set his tool belt on the front porch. He opened the rear of the long wagon and began pulling out the benches. He handed benches, two or three at a time, to his brothers, who toted them into the upper level of the white bank barn. In a couple of weeks, they would be repeating the motions at Isaiah's house, a short distance down the road. Isaiah's plans to marry Clara Ebersol and become the *daed* to two sets of irascible twins had been published the previous church Sunday. It hadn't been a surprise for anyone, because he and Clara had been taking care of the *kinder* since their parents' tragic deaths earlier in the year.

Daniel and his Hannah would be having their wedding before Christmas, giving the bride's relatives time to travel from New York State and other settlements to the west. They planned to keep the number of guests to a minimum because too much excitement would overwhelm her great-grandmother.

Micah would have been glad to work in silence, but his twin brother wouldn't have it. Daniel was happy to be in love, and he wanted everyone around him to feel the same.

"Have you talked to *Mamm* about whom you'll have the evening meal with?" Daniel asked as they toted a trio of stacked benches into the barn.

One of the favorite Amish traditions among newly married couples was arranging for their unwed guests to come into supper two by two and sit together through the evening. Courting couples dropped hints, so they would be matched. The rest were put together in the hope that the matchmaking would lead to them falling in love.

"No," Micah said in a tone he hoped his brother would realize meant the subject was closed.

Daniel either missed it or wanted to have his say. "You should talk to *Mamm* if there's someone special. Who knows? You could fall in love and get married, too."

"Love?" Micah sniffed his derision. "As far as I can see, there's not much difference between that and infatuation."

"Really?" Daniel grinned at him. "You haven't figured out the difference between them?"

"When did you?" he fired back, hating the envy pulsing through him that Daniel had won the woman of his dreams and Micah had failed twice.

"About ten seconds after Hannah slipped into my heart." His expression softened as he spoke of his fiancée. "Is this about Katie Kay?"

"You know we aren't supposed to talk about the person we're walking out with."

"You aren't walking out with her, though the two of you spend more time together than some married couples. When are you going to stop being a scaredy-cat and ask her to let you take her home?"

Knowing he had nothing to lose since Katie Kay had announced she wanted no more than friendship with him, he said, "I did. Last year."

Daniel's easy grin withered. "You never told me."

Micah realized he'd hurt his brother with his reticence. Growing up, the two of them had never had secrets from each other, and Daniel had been very upfront about falling in love with Hannah and her little sister and outspoken great-grandmother. Why hadn't he turned to his brother at the darkest point in his life?

"You were happy," he began and then halted himself before Daniel could reply. "No, that's not why I didn't say anything. I was humiliated when she told me to get lost. I didn't want to admit she'd dumped me."

"Because it would have made the breakup feel more final?"

"Ja." He sighed. "I've learned why pride is denounced. It leads a man to do things he normally wouldn't."

"You are beginning to grow up, bro."

"Bro?"

"You *are* my brother, aren't you?"

"You've been spending far too much time with *Eng-lischers*."

"And you've been spending a lot of time with Katie Kay from what I've heard. Why are you moping around? Because she's carrying another man's *bop-pli*? That didn't keep Joshua from marrying Rebekah."

Micah wanted to argue their oldest brother's situation had been very different. Rebekah's late husband had been Joshua's best friend, and Joshua had promised to look after her if something happened to Lloyd.

"It's complicated, Daniel," he said.

"Love is, but turning away from it is stupid. If you want it, you have to be willing to sacrifice everything to obtain it." Daniel walked out of the barn, leaving Micah to mull over his words.

The wedding was everything Micah could have wished for. It celebrated the love shared by *Mamm* and Reuben. All their *kinder* and *kins-kinder* were in attendance. A neighboring bishop listened to their vows to be with one another for the rest of their lives. Around the room, smiles broadened as the bride and groom returned to their seats after they were pronounced man and wife.

During the short wedding ceremony and the three-hour church service surrounding it, he'd been careful not to look in Katie Kay's direction. Envy wasn't an appealing emotion, and he didn't want her to see it on his face. Yet he couldn't help wishing he'd been the one, instead of Reuben, pledging to love one woman forever.

Don't be pathetic, he chided himself as he had often in the past week. Even if Katie Kay was ready to stay in their community, she had plenty of choices for a husband. He'd heard whispered comments from other bachelors while they waited to go into the house for the service. Some of the remarks had been unworthy of a God-fearing man because they derided Katie Kay's jumping the fence and then returning without having to be called to account in front of the *Leit* for her sins. Those fools needed to remember that that happened when a baptized member left and was put under the *bann*. The shunning wouldn't end until that person atoned for breaking his or her covenant with the Lord and with the congregation.

Most of the unmarried men, however, had announced they would willingly overlook Katie Kay's sojourn among the *Englischers* if she were to give them the slightest sign she was interested in one of them. None of them, of course, knew how she'd walked out with Micah and the single *wunderbaar* kiss they'd shared then.

Or the latest one.

With a sigh, he acknowledged nothing had changed. Katie Kay remained the focus of men's attention wherever she went. She wasn't ready to settle down, or at least not with him. If the other guys knew she was pregnant, would they change their minds?

You didn't. The small voice of truth answered him swiftly. But, for once, the little voice was wrong. He *had* changed his mind about Katie Kay since learning she was going to have a *boppli*. Not because of the unborn *kind*, but because he'd learned she was more than the flirt she'd portrayed well.

When the service was over, Micah gave *Mamm* a kiss on the cheek and shook Reuben's hand before moving aside to let others do the same. He glanced around the yard, where leaves had fallen to replace the ones they'd raked yesterday. Suddenly he felt more out of place than he had on the few trips he'd made with Sean into the city to meet with vendors.

He walked away from the happy guests, knowing he needed time to get his thoughts under control before he celebrated with friends, including the Donnellys, who'd been invited to the wedding dinner, and family...and Katie Kay.

The kitchen was busy with a half-dozen women who'd been asked to oversee the final preparation of the food for the wedding meal after the ceremony. Another group would step in and warm the leftovers for the evening meal. It was an honor to help for either meal, and Katie Kay was glad Wanda had picked her to work in the kitchen. It allowed her to keep a low profile.

If the other women had questions, they kept them to themselves as they worked to get food ready in time to serve three hundred guests. A few had been in the Stoltzfus kitchen since before dawn. Others, like Katie Kay, had joined them slicing bread and stirring chicken and stuffing after the exchange of vows.

Katie Kay was unwrapping sticks of butter to put on small plates, which would be placed on the tables by the young men and women acting as servers during the first seating. With so many guests, there would be at least three different servings.

"Let me help you," said a familiar voice in its usual icy tone.

Looking up, she saw her oldest sibling, Priscilla, carrying several more boxes of stick butter. Katie Kay said nothing as Priscilla set them on the table. They worked together in silence for several minutes.

Then Katie Kay said, "I owe you an apology, Priscilla. I haven't been fair to you."

"To me?" Her older sister stared at her in surprise that evolved into suspicion. "You've never worried about my feelings before."

"You're right. I've never worried about anyone's feelings but my own, because I was too wrapped up in my unhappiness to see beyond it."

"Why were you unhappy? Every boy in Paradise Springs and beyond wanted to walk out with you. Most of them probably still do. You don't have any reason to complain."

Katie Kay almost retorted that she wanted only one man to court her, but that was impossible now. She'd made such a muddle of everything. Micah had been honest with her the night she'd discovered she was pregnant. That night he'd told her he'd never ask her again to marry him. And why should he when she'd turned him down again?

She couldn't help pondering—for a moment—how different her life might have been if last year, she'd welcomed Micah's plans for their future instead of worrying about everything she might miss by spending the rest of her days with him.

Her sister didn't need to know how he'd planned a future with Katie Kay twice. Two very different futures but ones where they would have been together. As much as Katie Kay ached to heal the wounds between her and her far-too-perfect sister, there were embarrassing matters she had to keep to herself. She wanted to believe the best of Priscilla, but her sister enjoyed gossiping. Katie Kay wasn't going to give Priscilla more fodder by telling her about the biggest mistake of her life.

No. Not one mistake.

The *two* biggest mistakes of her life.

"I was unhappy," Katie Kay said in the same near-whisper, "because I knew I couldn't ever be you."

Priscilla opened her mouth to retort, but no sound came out as she stared at Katie Kay in disbelief. Swallowing hard, she managed to say, "I don't understand."

"I think you do. You made everything look easy, and you were never satisfied until whatever you were doing was perfect. How could I hope to emulate that after *Mamm* got sick and died? I can't cook as well as you. I can't sew as well as you, and I can't keep house as well as you."

"I thought you weren't interested in doing anything but having fun."

"I wanted to help *Daed* and the rest of the family." She heard the stove timer go off. She opened the oven door and lifted out a tray of rolls and tilted it so the rolls fell into one of the baskets beside the plates of butter. Setting another tray in the oven to warm, she added, "But I knew everyone was comparing me to you, and I was well aware how far I fell short of being the bishop's model daughter."

"Just as I did." Priscilla's voice lost its hard edge.

"You? You were perfect."

"Far from it. I know how everyone expects the bishop's *kinder* to be shining examples for their own families. Do you know why I tried hard to be perfect?"

"No." She'd never heard her older sister talk like this. "You made it look simple."

"It wasn't simple, but I learned how to pretend it was because I got tired of making mistakes and having everyone know. Maybe I've got too much *hochmut*, but I didn't want *Daed* to be disappointed in me like others were."

"I can't imagine anyone being disappointed in you."

"Do you think you're the only one who has gotten disappointed looks and tsk-tsks from people who think, no matter how hard you've tried, you can't measure up?"

Katie Kay stared at her sister. "Why didn't you say so after *Mamm* died and the responsibility for the house fell on my shoulders?"

"Because I was jealous of you," her sister answered as she opened another box of butter sticks.

"Of me? Why? I wasn't much more than a kid."

"You were filled with so much light and life you drew people to you like a moth to a flame. I used to be *Daed*'s precious little girl. That changed when you were born."

Katie Kay shook her head. "You're wrong. *Daed* doesn't have a favorite among us. If he did, it wouldn't be me because I've caused him many sleepless nights and heartache."

"You're asking me to explain something I don't understand myself." Priscilla stopped working, one of the few times Katie Kay had ever seen her hands idle. "Maybe I got lazy and didn't try to change a bad habit. Maybe I was resentful I had to leave behind my childhood when *Mamm* passed away, and everyone expected me to do the same again when your *mamm* died, though I was a new bride with a household of my own." Priscilla sighed before giving her an ironic smile. "I've been praying, Katie Kay, to discover why I reacted as I did after your *mamm* died. I wasn't ready to repeat those unhappy years in my life. I was sure there must be more—"

"Out there to experience," Katie Kay finished, hardly believing the words as she spoke of them.

"*Ja.* How did you know?"

"Maybe we were more alike than either of us has ever wanted to admit. I tried to be perfect…like you. And you wanted to find out about a life beyond the one you'd known as the bishop's daughter…like I did when I jumped the fence."

"Have you jumped back?"

"Ja." She put her fingers over her burgeoning abdomen. "I've got to think of someone else besides myself."

"Do you realize our *bopplin* will be born within weeks of each other?"

"You're pregnant?"

Priscilla nodded, her face brightening. "I found out yesterday. I plan to tell *Daed* and Wanda tomorrow. Today is for them. But our little ones will be cousins and can grow up together if you stay here."

"That would be *wunderbaar*." Katie Kay hugged her sister and meant it for the first time in longer than she could remember. Maybe her whole life. It was sad to think of the times they might have had together if they had talked years ago as they were now.

As the day unfolded, Katie Kay couldn't help looking for Micah. She spoke with his brothers and his sisters and their spouses and *kinder*, but each time she saw him at a distance, he was gone before she could reach the spot. Was he avoiding her? She couldn't blame him, but she'd thought he would give her the chance to apologize. At least one more time.

She found him among the young people gathering to be matched to eat supper together. It was a tradition those who were walking out together loved and everyone else endured. She wondered what Micah was feeling when he was instructed to stand by her side.

He said nothing, so she struggled to find a way to

break the silence between them. Anything she could think of to say sounded insipid in her mind. Taking his hands in hers and pleading with him to let her explain her poor choice of words was impossible when other people milled around them.

By the time they were seated at one of the tables, she still hadn't found the right words. She was relieved when Micah asked without looking at her, "It was a nice wedding, ain't so?"

"A wedding where two people are in love with each other is a reason for celebration." She fought not to frown at her words, which were as trite as his. Not wanting to let the silence smother them again, she asked, "Did the Donnellys enjoy themselves?"

"As much as they could when most of the people around them were speaking *Deitsch*. I arranged for them to be part of the first seating, because the kids aren't used to waiting to eat as ours are."

"I had barely enough time to say hi to them. Olivia looks better, don't you think?"

"Sean says she's tired of not being able to run around with her brothers. If she does too much, the cough returns. The *doktor* wants her to take it easy for another week." At last a smile pulled at his lips. "Gemma says she doesn't know if she can put up with Olivia's complaining that long."

"I let Gemma know she can ask me to babysit whenever she needs a break."

"That's generous of you, Katie Kay."

"It's nothing compared to what they did for me."

He rested his elbow on the table and leaned toward her. "Does this mean you're staying in Paradise Springs?"

Before she could answer, the roar of a car without a

muffler exploded through the evening. The black car sped up the farm lane and squealed to a stop behind the rearmost buggy. Katie Kay's sharp intake of breath sounded like a shout in her ears, but only Micah seemed to notice. He put his hand over hers beneath the table as everyone stared at the car and the brown-haired man getting out of it.

Her whisper was as loud as a shout in the shocked silence. "Austin!"

Chapter Sixteen

Katie Kay gripped the table. She continued to stare at Austin, whom she'd hoped never to see again. If she'd imagined talking to him another time, it certainly wouldn't have been in the midst of *Daed*'s and Wanda's wedding supper.

He was dressed in casual *Englisch* style. Well-worn blue jeans, his favorite cowboy boots he wore though she doubted he'd ever been on a horse, and a dark blue T-shirt beneath his gray hoodie. His brown eyes scanned the crowd as he paused in the barn's doorway, and he began to smile when his gaze found hers. Strolling toward her as if he were the master of everything around him, he preened beneath the stares.

Her heart contracted in dismay and fear at what he might say and do. Why did he have to come and chance ruining *Daed*'s wedding? Was his arrival a horrible coincidence, or had Cherokee mentioned something to Vinnie, who then blabbed to Austin?

She wouldn't put such grandstanding past him, but she shouldn't paint him with misdeeds he hadn't done... yet. She needed to keep him from having the opportunity to make one of the scenes he loved. Could she convince him to talk to her privately? That way, he wouldn't intrude further on the wedding.

"You know him?" her *daed* asked as he came to stand next to her chair.

"Ja." She wanted to look at Micah to see his reaction, but she didn't dare to pull her eyes from Austin's broadening smile. Instantly she knew he was hoping to cause as much trouble as possible.

"You don't look happy to see him."

"It's all right, *Daed*," she said. "I'll handle it."

"You know him?" asked Ina Sue from the other side of the table. She put her hand over her mouth as comprehension bloomed in her eyes and the eyes of everyone else who knew about the *boppli*.

Wanda reached over and took her hand and gave it a gentle squeeze as she whispered, "God is with us always, my dear daughter. Don't forget that. You are never alone."

"I know." A strength that came from the depths of her heart, the part she'd kept closed, startled her, but she was grateful for how it allowed her to straighten her shoulders and raise her chin. Not in pride, but in knowing she was loved by the Lord and her family and her community. All of them were holding her up as she crossed the barn toward Austin.

"Hey, baby," he said as she came closer. "You're looking pretty good for—"

Putting her hand on his arm, she didn't let him finish because she was sure he'd use one of his crude terms. He considered plain folk backward and too stupid to become part of the twenty-first century.

Suddenly she was ashamed. Not for herself, but for Austin, who believed, in order for people to notice him, he had to create trouble wherever he went. No wonder she'd been drawn into his life after they first met. She'd enjoyed attention as he still did. They were an imperfect match, the *Englisch* slacker who felt the world owed him a living and the Amish girl who'd believed the wider world owed her a whirl of excitement.

"Let's talk somewhere private," she said.

"I don't want to—"

Her fingers curled around his arm. "Either *komm* with me or leave."

"Hey, you're sounding Amish again. Did you forget how to talk good English?"

Before he could say more to insult her family and their friends, she tugged him away from the tables and out of the barn so what they said wouldn't be heard by others. Even if he threw a tantrum as he'd done more than once.

Austin made a pretense of protesting and then went along. Why wouldn't he when he was getting what he wanted? He had her full attention.

Leaning against the stone foundation of the tall barn, he chuckled. "Honey, I know you want to get me alone. Out behind the barn?" He gave her a wink.

"What are you doing here?"

"Cherokee told Vinnie you hadn't decided yet to get rid of the kid after it's born, so I figured I'd come out and see your glow of impending motherhood. And I thought I'd make sure you remembered you need to give me my share of whatever money the adoptive parents give you." With a coarse laugh, he said, "I hear you country girls like to entertain in the hayloft. Want to show me?"

She ignored the coarse words he obviously thought were seductive. It was impossible not to compare him to Micah, who was always solicitous of her. Micah treated everyone with kindness and respect. He'd been as concerned about Gemma's health while Olivia was in the hospital as Sean was.

"Austin, I think you should leave."

"But I just got here. You're not going to send me away without a plate of that great-smelling food and a piece of the wedding cake, are you?"

"You weren't invited."

He waved aside her words. "Don't split hairs with me. How many times did you tell me about how the Amish share what they've got to eat with anyone who stops in at mealtime?"

She started to answer, but a deeper voice said from around the corner of the barn, "She's asked you to leave."

Whirling, she saw Micah walking toward them. To judge by his easy pace, he was mildly perturbed, but she saw anger snapping in his eyes. She wanted to caution him about Austin's temper. Anything he said could make the situation worse…if that was possible because the very air seemed to hum with tension.

"Who's this loser?" sneered Austin.

"I'm Micah Stoltzfus," he said before she could answer.

Austin glanced at her. "Your ex?"

"*You* are my ex, Austin," Katie Kay said, trying to copy Micah's cool serenity. "You became my ex when you pushed me out of your car on a cold, rainy night after stealing my money and cell phone. I should have sent the police to arrest you." In spite of her efforts, her voice began to tremble with the emotions she was struggling to control.

A gentle hand settled on her waist, out of Austin's sight. Micah's touch offered her strength. Though she longed to turn and throw her arms around him and ask him to forgive her for how she'd hurt him, she continued to look at Austin.

"It was a mistake," he said in the whining tone he used whenever he tried to get what he wanted.

She wasn't going to be taken in again. Her voice was steady when she replied, "Finally something we agree on."

"We can have good times again, Sweetie-Kate," he said, using the nickname he seemed to recall whenever he wanted to wheedle her into going along with his latest scheme. "I've got almost enough money to buy the motorcycle I told you about. We can head anywhere we want." His nose wrinkled as he glanced at Micah. "You don't have to stay around this place that reeks of cow manure and dumb-dumb Dutch."

She was tempted to tell Austin he was wrong if he thought trying to offend Micah would get the usual reaction. Micah wasn't going to answer with either words or fists.

"No, thank you," she said. "My family and my life are in Paradise Springs."

"But I know you want to see the world. You said so yourself a dozen times. I'll get the bike, and we'll hit the road and see it."

"What about our *kind*—our child?" she amended when she realized he wouldn't recognize the *Deitsch* word.

Austin waved aside her question. "If the kid is a problem," he said, "we'll figure something out. There are always people looking for a baby, no questions asked." He smiled as if he'd come up with the perfect solution.

Behind Katie Kay, Micah took a deep breath to restrain himself from reaching out and grabbing the loudmouth by the front of his T-shirt. Never had he been so furious. Not even when Katie Kay told him to be on his way and not return.

Stay with me, Lord, and help me remember nothing is solved by losing my temper.

A gentle peace settled around his heart, easing the tightness that had tormented him since he last walked out with Katie Kay. All that time, though he'd tried to deny it, he'd been angry. But anger solved nothing. It only separated him from God. He had to let go of the rage and begin to offer forgiveness.

Offer forgiveness to himself and to Katie Kay. He had to forgive himself for pushing her too hard and too fast…as Austin was. And forgive her for pushing back as she fought to discover what she wanted. Not what he wanted or what Austin wanted or her *boppli*, but what life she wanted. He'd made the decision for himself, and she deserved the same chance to choose.

Using only words an *Englischer* would understand, he said, "A baby isn't something to 'figure out.' A baby is a precious gift from God, and he or she should be treasured, not seen as an inconvenience."

"Why don't you stay out of this, farm boy?" He jutted his chin toward Micah in a candid invitation to take a swing. "It's none of your business."

"You're right," Micah said in the same composed tone, not taking the bait. He was aware of the many eyes witnessing this confrontation from a distance. Most of the guests, including his brothers and brothers-in-law, had moved to where they could watch. A single signal from him, and they would step forward as a unified force, but he didn't want that. He wasn't tempted to sink to Austin's level. There was desperation in the man's voice, and Micah wasn't going to feed that. "It is none of my business, except for the fact that Katie Kay is part of our community, and so is her *boppli*. Her baby."

"You don't know she's going to stay." His voice rose in volume on every word as if he could intimidate Micah by yelling.

The man was a bully.

Micah looked at him without replying. Anything he said would be thrown in his face and prolong the conversation.

When Austin realized Micah wasn't going to retort, he poked a finger in Katie Kay's direction. "You escaped from this straitlaced world once, Sweetie-Kate. Let me help you put it behind you forever."

"Forever?" When she widened her eyes and batted her lashes, Micah had to struggle not to laugh. He'd seen her do the same when an overly eager young man tried to impress her after a singing. "Are you proposing, Austin?"

The *Englischer* choked out a curse and shook his head like a dog coming out of water. "I didn't say anything about marriage."

"No, you didn't. And why would you? You don't want to grow up and take on a man's responsibilities. You want to have fun while you convince your friends to support you, as you convinced me to do. I was a fool, but I'm not going to be a fool any longer."

Quietly, too quietly for Austin to hear, Micah murmured, "Fool me once, shame on you. Fool me twice, shame on me."

She took his hand. When he laced his fingers through hers, he watched as her shoulders rose as if she'd rid herself of a heavy burden.

"I think you should leave, Austin," Katie Kay said. "Leave and don't return."

"Oh, I'll be coming back." He pointed at her stomach. "It's *my* baby! Don't think I'm going to let you keep it! You wait and see."

When she didn't answer, he strode away, his feet pounding the ground as if he could make his footsteps echo across the valley. The wedding guests parted like the Red Sea to let him pass, but nobody spoke when he snarled at them. He got in his car and disappeared into a cloud of leaf debris and dust.

He was gone.

At last.

Micah saw Katie Kay shaking, and he wanted to help her, but wasn't sure what to say. Would Austin try to take her *boppli* from her? Maybe he thought Amish people didn't use attorneys. They didn't often, but when a *kind*'s life was at stake, he knew Reuben would give permission to hire legal assistance.

When his fingers settled on her shoulders, he was startled. She wasn't trembling with fear or with anger.

She was *laughing*?

As if he'd asked out loud, she smiled at him. "Well, you got your wish. You got to meet Austin and give him a piece of your mind."

"He needs more than a piece if he thinks he can threaten to take your *boppli* from you. A couple of my brothers have adopted *kinder*. The attorney they used—"

She put a finger to his lips. "Let's not look for trouble before it arrives."

"That sounds like the old Katie Kay, the one who didn't want to think beyond the moment she was in."

"No, I'm thinking beyond the moment, but nothing is going to happen until after this *boppli* is born in about six months." Folding her hands behind her, she looked into his eyes. "Until then, I plan to stay in Paradise Springs. It's the best place for me and my *boppli.*"

"It's a big change of heart, Katie Kay."

"*Ja*, it is." A smile drifted outward from the corners of her lips. "I've had several changes of heart in the past few days. You may not believe it, but Priscilla and I have come to an understanding."

"You have?" His eyes widened. He hadn't expected that after many years of acrimony between them.

"She's my family, and after seeing how Sean and Gemma and their *kinder* treasure each other, I realized I wanted to treasure my family, too."

"Your *boppli* needs a family, Katie Kay."

"I know, and he or she will have one. *Daed* and Wanda have shown me how eager they are to hold my little one in their arms."

"*My* little one? It's the first time I've heard you say that."

"Maybe because I've come to see I would be a fool to miss a moment with my *boppli*. My *mamm* is with the Lord and watches over me, but since I've learned I'm going to have a *kind* myself, I know she would have been grateful to have more time with my sisters and me." She curved her hand over her belly, where her *boppli* was growing, before looking at him again. "I know you've been curious about the main reason I jumped the fence."

"*Ja.*"

"It was because I was in love with you."

He was about to laugh and then realized she was serious. "In love?" He pointed at her and then himself. "You were in love with me? You sure had a strange way of showing that."

"I was scared, Micah. Scared of how I felt when I was with you."

"How did you feel?"

Her eyes glowed with powerful emotions. "As if, with you, I had everything I ever wanted or needed."

"But…"

She put her finger to his lips to silence him. "I was scared because I wondered if there was something more for me out in the *Englisch* world. I didn't want to come to regret that I had never found out if there was."

"And what did you find?"

"I was a fool to worry about missing out on something I couldn't name when you were offering me everything."

He drew her into his arms and rested his cheek on top of her *kapp*. "I'm sorry, Katie Kay, for pushing you into a corner."

"What do you have to be sorry for? All you did was make me fall in love with you."

Could he be any happier than he was at the moment when she told him she loved him? He got his answer when she smiled and said, "I love you, Micah Stoltzfus. Will you marry me?"

He chuckled. "You, the girl, are asking me, the boy? You never do things the way other people do them, ain't so?"

"Ja." Her fingers swept along his cheek and into his hair, her touch gentle and yet sending shivers through him that threatened to buckle his knees. "You said that you'd never ask me again. I love you and want to spend my life with you and have you be my *boppli*'s *daed*, so I'm asking you. Marry me, Micah. Do you love me?"

"With every bit of my heart. *Ja*, my love, I will marry

you." He pulled her into his arms and found her lips with the ease of months of longing to hold her.

She jerked back and gasped, "Oh!" Her fingers were splayed across her abdomen.

"Katie Kay, are you all right?"

Joy glowed from her as she whispered, "I felt the *boppli* move."

"You did? What does it feel like?"

She grasped his hand and pressed it against her. A faint sensation fluttered against his palm.

In awe, he cupped her face and bent to kiss her, knowing it would be the first of many kisses they'd share in the years to come.

Epilogue

$\backsim$

Snow fell outside, but the cozy kitchen was warm. Katie Kay leaned over the cradle and smiled at the tiny bundle in it. Soft curls were so blond they appeared white, and the little girl's blue eyes were closed while her mouth worked as if tasting the air.

"You are *wunderbaar*, Sarann," she whispered. She didn't want to wake the *boppli* named for her beloved younger sister.

Unlike her sister, her daughter, Sarann, appeared to be healthy in every way. Beth Ann had insisted on having a *doktor* present at the birth at the house Micah had purchased a couple of months after he exchanged vows with Katie Kay. *Doktorfraa* Montgomery had checked Sarann and pronounced she showed no sign of any genetic disorders or other problems. When Sarann had let out a loud cry at that moment, they'd laughed.

Including Micah, who'd offered to be with Katie Kay for the delivery, giving her back massages to ease the labor pains. No one mentioned that the *boppli* wasn't his, and he'd been thrilled with the little girl. He'd cradled her while Beth Ann tended to Katie Kay, and he mumbled nonsense like any new *daed*.

And he was Sarann's *daed* in everything but name.

"We are blessed, little one, to have such a man love us."

She looked around the kitchen, awed by the gifts heaped upon her by their loving God. The room had been painted a light blue with white wainscoting before Sarann's arrival, while Katie Kay still had been able to go up a ladder. The gas stove was a hand-me-down, but the refrigerator was new, a gift from her *daed* and Micah's *mamm*. Dishes that once had belonged to her own *mamm* were drying in the rack by the sink.

The house needed work, but it had five *gut*-sized bedrooms and three bathrooms as well as an artesian well in the cellar and storage in the attic. A chicken coop was close to the stable, which was large enough to hold two horses and the family buggy Micah had traded his courting buggy for after their wedding.

Peeling wallpaper and chipped paint would be taken care of. Between Micah and his brothers and Sean, who insisted on giving a hand now that his new son was almost six months old, the house was already much more livable than it'd been when Micah and Katie Kay had first seen it.

The door opened, and cold air and snowflakes floated in. Micah shook snow off his hat before he hung it on the peg by the door.

"How's our girl?" he asked.

Standing, Katie Kay smiled. "She's doing great. Sleeping like a pro."

He chuckled and then grew serious. "I stopped at the mailbox. Here."

She took the manila envelope he held out to her. When she saw the official return address, she eagerly turned it over and opened it. She pulled out a thick collection of papers. Paging through, she found the one she was looking for. She plucked it out and let the others fall on the table beside her. She found Austin's signature scrawled at the bottom.

"Is it settled?" Micah asked.

"Austin signed his parental rights away, as I'd prayed he would." She raised her eyes to Micah's, knowing they could complete the paperwork for him to adopt Sarann and become her legal *daed*. "You don't look surprised."

"I'm not. As soon as your friend Cherokee told you Austin had bought the motorcycle he was talking about, I knew he wouldn't want to be slowed down by a *boppli*."

"What about you, Micah?" She tossed the page on top of the others, knowing she'd read every word later. "Are you afraid of being slowed down by Sarann and me?"

"No, because no matter where we go and how we get there, we'll always be side by side. You and me and our daughter and any other *kinder* the *gut* Lord blesses us with."

She put her arm around his waist as he slid his around her shoulders. Together they looked at the *boppli*, knowing they both had the life they'd wanted, despite their roundabout way of discovering it. They had a life filled with love.

A life together.

* * * * *

Dear Reader,

Dorothy isn't the only one who wonders what's "over the rainbow." That song and story resonate with us because we're impatient to find out what lies ahead or want to make sure, as Katie Kay does, that we're not missing out on something important. Learning to "let go and let God" is tough, and many of us have to learn it over and over. And sometimes the hard way. With each reminder that God understands what's truly inside her, Katie Kay opens her heart to Him and love. And that's a lesson for all of us to let go and let God lead us on the path He has for us, isn't it?

Stop in and visit me at *www.joannbrownbooks.com*. Look for my next story coming soon from Harlequin Love Inspired.

Wishing you many blessings,
Jo Ann Brown

Get 2 Free Books,

Plus 2 Free Gifts—

just for trying the Reader Service!

All Miranda Morgan wants for Christmas is to be a good mom to the twins she's been named guardian of—but their brooding cowboy godfather, Simon West, isn't sure she's ready. Can they learn to trust in each other and become a real family for the holidays?

Read on for a sneak peek of
TEXAS CHRISTMAS TWINS
by **Deb Kastner**,
part of the **CHRISTMAS TWINS** miniseries.

"I brought you up here because I have a couple of dogs I'd especially like to introduce to Harper and Hudson," he said.

She flashed him a surprised look. He couldn't possibly think that with all she had going on, she'd want to adopt a couple of dogs, or even one.

"I appreciate what you do here," she said, trying to buffer her next words. "But I want to make it clear up front that I have no intention of adopting a dog. They're cute and all, but I've already got my hands full with the twins as it is."

"Oh, no," Simon said, raising his free hand, palm out. "You misunderstand me. I'm not pulling some sneaky stunt on you to try to get you to adopt a dog. It's just that—well, maybe it would be easier to show you than to try to explain."

"Zig! Zag! Come here, boys." Two identical small white dogs dashed to Simon's side, their full attention on him.

Miranda looked from one dog to the other and a light bulb went off in her head.

"Twins!" she exclaimed.

Simon laughed.

"Not exactly. They're littermates."

He helped an overexcited Harper pet one of the dogs and, taking Simon's lead, Miranda helped Hudson scratch the ears of the other.

"Soft fur, see, Harper?" Simon said. "This is a doggy."

"Gentle, gentle," Miranda added when Hudson tried to grab a handful of the white dog's fur.

"Zig and Zag are Westies—West Highland white terriers."

Zig licked Hudson's fist and he giggled. Both dogs seemed to like the babies, and the twins were clearly taken with the dogs.

But she'd meant what she'd said earlier—no dogs allowed. At the moment, suffering cuteness overload, she even had to give herself a stern mental reminder.

She cast her eyes up to make sure Simon understood her very emphatic message, but he was busy helping Harper interact with Zag.

When he finally looked up, their eyes met and locked. A slow smile spread across his lips and appreciation filled his gaze. For a moment, Miranda experienced something she hadn't felt this strongly since, well, since high school—the reel of her stomach in time with a quickened pulse and a shortness of breath.

Either she was having an asthma attack, or else—

She was absolutely not going to go there.

Don't miss
TEXAS CHRISTMAS TWINS
by Deb Kastner, available December 2017 wherever
Love Inspired® books and ebooks are sold.

www.LoveInspired.com

New York Times **bestselling author**

SHERRYL WOODS

delivers a brand-new story in her beloved Chesapeake Shores series in an epic return you won't want to miss!

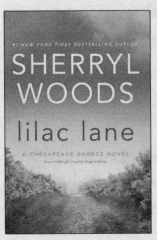

After her fiancé suffers a fatal heart attack, Keira Malone is grieving and unsure of what's next. She moves from Dublin to Chesapeake Shores, Maryland, to spend time with her daughter, Moira, and her new granddaughter, Kate, as well as to help her son-in-law, Luke, with his Irish pub, O'Briens.

She rents a charming cottage on Lilac Lane, replete with views of the ocean and her neighbor's thriving garden. The neighbor is none other than Bryan Laramie, the brusque and moody chef at the pub. Things get real when Bryan's long-lost daughter shows up out of the blue. As Bryan and Keira each delve into their pasts, the rest of the town is gearing up for the Fall Festival Irish Stew cook-off, and making no bones about whose side they're on. A recipe for disaster...or a new take on love?

Available October 17, wherever books are sold!

Love Inspired®

**Inspirational Romance to
Warm Your Heart and Soul**

Join our social communities to connect
with other readers who share your love!

Sign up for the Love Inspired newsletter
at **www.LoveInspired.com** to be the
first to find out about upcoming titles,
special promotions and exclusive content.

CONNECT WITH US AT:

Harlequin.com/Community

 Facebook.com/LoveInspiredBooks

 Twitter.com/LoveInspiredBks